PIXEL

To: HALEY

WITH LOTS OF LOVE

FROM GRANDMA !

JULY, 2013

PIXEL

ARTHUR HUGHES

authorHOUSE®

AuthorHouse™
1663 Liberty Drive
Bloomington, IN 47403
www.authorhouse.com
Phone: 1-800-839-8640

Published by AuthorHouse   03/16/2013

ISBN: 978-1-4772-8160-4 (sc)
ISBN: 978-1-4772-8159-8 (e)

Library of Congress Control Number: 2012919507

PROLOGUE

The year 1776 was a very special year for Americans. It was the year that their country became an independent nation. It was also a special year for the people who lived on a small planet called Larth. It was in 1776 that a spaceship from planet Larth arrived on our planet.

The people of Larth looked just like the people of Earth, except that they were very small. Most of the adults were only one inch tall. But in 1776 they knew more science than we did. They knew that there were living things on our planet, and they wanted to find out how intelligent these creatures might be.

Their scientists built a spacecraft that could travel to Earth. But they had serious problems. The engine was not powerful enough to overcome Earth's gravity, and the spacecraft was only large enough for one person. The scientists needed a volunteer who would travel to Earth knowing that he or she would never be able to return to their home planet.

The chief scientist, who developed the spacecraft, wanted to be the one to go to Earth. But the people in charge of the space program felt that the chief scientist was needed to develop more powerful engines for future missions.

The chief scientist's son, Pixel, knew a lot about the space program and he asked his Dad if he could be the volunteer to go to Earth. Of course his Dad and Mom were very upset that their son wanted to go on such a dangerous mission. But they agreed readily; they knew that some Larthan son or daughter would have to go, and they were proud of their son for volunteering.

Pixel was the solitary passenger on the spacecraft that arrived on Earth in 1776. He was to become Larth's greatest hero.

LANDING

As the spacecraft orbited closer to Earth, Pixel was amazed at the vast quantity of water that covered the planet. Of course he had made many orbits of his own planet, to test the spacecraft, and he loved the beauty of Larth. But the size and beauty of Earth was truly awesome.

During each orbit cameras on the spacecraft recorded details of Earth's surface. On-board computers created a 3d global image of Earth that was continuously updated during each orbit. After sixty days of orbiting Pixel had a good understanding of Earth's geography. As the orbits got closer and closer to Earth he could recognize many large cities; there were intelligent creatures on Earth. What would they be like? Would he be able to communicate with them? How intelligent were they? Would they be peaceful?

Pixel decided to land the spacecraft on a continent that seemed to be much less developed than others. It was a continent that had cities and towns clustered close to an enormous sea. Inland from the coastal cities was a vast forest that appeared to be uninhabited. But should he land on water or ground? The space craft was designed for either landing. He would have liked to discuss this problem with Mission Control, but his reports now took over three years to reach Larth. In the very early weeks of the journey he had been able to talk directly to his Dad at Mission Control but now he had to make all decisions on his own. He decided that water would be safer and guided the spacecraft to a large lake, far from the towns on the sea coast.

The tiny spacecraft was engulfed by huge waves as soon as it splashed into the lake. Pixel was no longer in control. Flotation devices, like huge tires, were automatically deployed so that the spacecraft could float safely on the waves. This gave Pixel time to actuate the helicopter style rotors and fly the spacecraft to the nearest shore.

The trees were enormous. He flew the spacecraft to the tops of the highest trees and looked, with wonder and fear, at an unending sea of green.

Pixel wanted to find a location where he could explore outside the spacecraft without encountering the intelligent creatures who lived on the planet. He circled a very wide area of the forest to ensure that there were no towns or settlements close to the area he planned to explore. He encountered huge birds, almost as large as the spacecraft, circling the forests. They were so intent on their search for game that it seemed to Pixel that they did not notice the spacecraft. They were certainly not the creatures who created the towns on the coast. But they were massive compared to the birds on Larth.

He found a wide valley of towering trees that was remote from any settlement of intelligent creatures. He landed the spacecraft on a high cliff overlooking the valley.

His on-board testing of the atmosphere had confirmed that he could breathe the air of the planet. He had a gravity control belt that would enable him to fly, or hover, using controls attached to his wrist. The equipment had been tested on Larth, but would it work on Earth? Pixel stood in the controlled exit area of the spacecraft, and opened the hatch. He could breathe. The air had a fine pine smell, and was fresh and delightful! He stepped from the exit ramp, activated the gravity controls, and soared above the trees. He felt free and exhilarated as he glided, and turned, trying to imitate the huge birds, but lacking their grace. Still, he could fly.

FIRST CONTACT

Pixel slept very soundly on his first night on Earth. He was in a deep sleep when he heard the spacecraft's alarm system signaling danger. As he leapt from his bed he could feel a violent shaking of the spacecraft. He glanced at the TV monitor and saw that a huge bird was trying to nudge the spacecraft off the side of the cliff! He quickly started the solar powered engine and the vibrations of the spacecraft frightened the bird into flight.

In moments the spacecraft was also in the air and Pixel realized that in future he would have to be very careful in choosing where to park. He flew the spacecraft eastward towards the towns on the seacoast. He hovered high above a large coastal city. Too high to see creatures on the ground but it was clear that the buildings were not unlike buildings on Larth. It was also clear that these creatures did not have flying machines because he had not seen any in the skies as he circled the town. He was afraid to fly lower until he learned more about the intelligent creatures who lived in these towns. It would be safer if he explored the remote farms, inland from the coastal cities, where he would encounter fewer creatures. Pixel flew the spacecraft westward from the sea until he reached an isolated farm, on the edge of the vast forest.

He landed the spacecraft at the opening of a large cave near the secluded farm. Wearing his anti-gravity suit he hovered to the back of the cavern and, with the aid of a powerful searchlight, he determined that there were no Earth creatures in the cavern. Using his hand held solar power pack Pixel moved several large rocks on the cavern floor to create a fairly level area to park the spacecraft. He then activated the warning system so that the spacecraft would take flight if its motion detectors sensed a large life form approaching. Satisfied that the spacecraft was secure, Pixel flew out of the cavern and headed for the settlements.

He was soon hovering high over an isolated cabin. As he drifted lower he could see earth creatures in the cultivated field outside the cabin. He decided to approach them by flying through the trees in the forest. The trees were so high and wide that it was very easy to fly through the gaps between them, until he was very close to the cabin. When he flew into the open field surrounding the cabin, he was in sight of the Earth creatures.

They were giants! Giants in size, but in looks exactly like the people of Larth!

Pixel was too afraid to get any closer. He flew to the highest tree close to the cabin, landed on a branch, and hid within a cluster of leaves. He could observe the earthlings without being seen. He was not alone in the trees. There were large birds on the branches, not the size of the ones on the cliff, but certainly larger than Pixel. The birds seemed to be oblivious to Pixel's presence in the trees. They ignored him as they flew from branch to branch.

There were three giants working in the field. They had no machines. The largest earthling, (Pixel assumed it was the mother) was digging with a shovel in a vegetable garden. A smaller earthling, a boy, was cutting down small trees with an axe, near the edge of the forest. A girl, the smallest earthling, was just standing by her mother, talking excitedly. Pixel was sure that they could not see him, because he was so small. To get a better look he glided to the roof of the cabin. The cabin was made of logs, but the joints were quite crude, making it easy to climb through a space between logs to look inside.

It was very dark. There were no windows in the cabin; the only light came from the doorway. It was very primitive compared to the sleek homes on Larth. Pixel looked down from inside the roof of the cabin to a bunk bed covered with blankets. There was a fireplace in one corner of the room, with dying embers from a wood fire. The only furniture in the room was a wooden table, four rustic chairs, and several wooden chests. The family was poor.

Pixel hovered gently to the bunk bed, and landed on a ladder that led to the ground floor. He was startled when the youngest earthling burst into the cabin. He ducked into the folds of the blanket, and watched as the earthling opened one of the chests. She had a basket of eggs, and she carefully placed each egg in the wooden chest. Just as quickly as she appeared she was gone.

Pixel was very nervous. He would have to be much more vigilant in future. He hovered back to the top of the cabin, just over the door, and found another space to crawl through. He now had a good view of a shed where the smallest earthling was feeding chickens. She was collecting more eggs for the chest in the cabin. Since all Larthans are vegetarians Pixel did not realize that the eggs being collected were actually food for the earthlings. Animals are not kept in captivity on Larth so Pixel found it strange that the non-flying birds were imprisoned in a cage. There was much to learn. But he was very concerned that he might be detected by the giants. He decided to return to the spaceship to send a complete report to Mission Control. No one on Larth had imagined that the planet would be a land of giants!

ABC

The next morning Pixel flew directly to the cabin. He brought with him a video recorder that would save digital images that could be transmitted from the spacecraft back to Larth.

It was another beautiful spring day. All three giants were outside the cabin so Pixel found a perch in the roof overlooking the farm. He began to video the youngest giant in the chicken run. She was feeding the chickens that were clucking noisily as they clustered around her. She collected eggs from the chicken coops, and then she played with the baby chicks. These would be delightful images for Mission Control. Larth had a system of interconnected computers that was similar to our internet. Pixel could imagine the pleasure of all Larthans when they saw, on their home monitors, his videos of the giants.

He videoed the mother as she worked her vegetable garden, and when she came into the cabin to rekindle the fire and prepare a soup for lunch. He videoed the family having soup at their solitary table. Their happy chatter was also recorded, but of course the words had no meaning for Pixel.

That night, back at the spacecraft, he considered how he might learn the language of the giants. He knew that experts on Larth would be able to decipher the language if he sent them enough recordings. But he also realized that he would have to wait for many years before Mission Control would provide him with help. In the mean time he knew that providing Mission Control with daily recordings would be very important. To get more recordings he decided that he should spend a night in the cabin.

When Pixel returned the next evening the mother was busy preparing supper on a wood burning fire. From a niche in the roof, directly over the kitchen table, he started his recordings.

"We shall be going to town tomorrow," the mother said. "Sally, please prepare your eggs for the trip. Make sure there are enough feathers in the bag so that no eggs are broken this time."

"I will mother," said Sally. She opened one of the chests, and Pixel saw that it was filled with eggs, in a bed of feathers.

"Can I help you, mother?" asked Adam.

"Yes, Adam, you should bring in some more wood for the fire."

Pixel continued his recording through supper, until candles were lit and the mother started knitting. "Time to practice writing, Sally. And Adam, please help your sister."

"Yes, mother." said Adam. "Sally I want you to write the words—'please help me', with a capital P."

Sally picked up a flat black slate and wrote the words—'Pleas help me.'

"That's fine Sally," said Adam. "But the word 'please' needs another 'e' at the end.

With a small cloth Sally erased the word—'pleas' and wrote—'please' instead. She continued practicing on her slate for over an hour, with much help from Adam. The light from the candles was so dim that Pixel climbed down to the bunk bed to get a better image of the writing tablet.

"Time for bed, Sally. And say your prayers."

"Can we sing first, Mom?" And before her mother could answer, Sally was singing joyously, joined immediately by her brother and mother.

"Off to bed now, darling, and don't forget your prayers."

Pixel was startled to see Sally bounding up the ladder. He tried to run to the nearest wall, but tripped in the blanket, just as Sally climbed onto the bed. He was almost crushed when Sally kneeled to say her prayers. But as she closed her eyes and whispered a few words Pixel was able to crawl out of the blanket and climb the wall of the cabin. He found a niche in the dark roof and resumed his video recording. The mother and son were quiet while Sally went to sleep.

Pixel felt a deep longing for his own family as he watched the giants, peaceful in candlelight. He returned to the spaceship, and while the videos were being transmitted to Mission Control, he wished he could talk directly with his Dad. He would tell him of his loneliness, and of the warmth and love that he saw in his family of giants.

PRISONER

Pixel could not find the family when he returned the next morning; they were not in the cabin or in the fields. He circled the settlements close to the cabin, but they could not be found. Finally he flew towards a small collection of buildings that seemed to be the centre of the community ; it was several hours walking distance from the cabin. He found the family walking down a dirt track towards the general store. Sally was in front, with two woven, egg filled baskets draped over her shoulders. Adam and his mother also had baskets of eggs.

When they entered the store Pixel flew through a window on the second floor into a large store room. From the staircase he could see the mother talking to the shopkeeper.

"Good day, Mary," said the shopkeeper. "I see that Sally has collected lots of eggs."

"Yes, Mr. Brown," said the mother. "Sally loves working with the chickens. She is a great help to me. I would like some sugar and flour today."

Sally was looking at herself in a large mirror near the front of the store. They had no mirrors in their cabin, and Sally was entranced with her image. Adam was looking at books. The store was also the local library and Adam was looking for *Robinson Crusoe*, a novel by Daniel Defoe.

"I found *Robinson Crusoe*, mother. Can I really have it?" asked Adam.

"I promised you, son. But remember you will have to read it aloud to Sally. Bring it to Mr. Brown. He needs to record it in his lending note book. And Sally, it's time for us to go."

On the way home the family stopped at the blacksmith's yard to look at the horses.

"Will we ever get a horse, Mom?" Adam asked. "It would really help us on the farm."

"You know we need to clear a lot more land, Adam, before we think about horses. In any event I would like a cow first. We will just have to work a little harder," his mother replied, as she smiled, and hugged his shoulders. "You will have a horse, soon enough."

Pixel watched the family walk down the main street, and then into a wide track that led through fields of corn. Pixel knew that the family would take several hours to walk to the cabin so he flew ahead to set up the night's video recording. Pixel was concerned that Mission Control might not be able to decipher the images from Sally's slate. Inside the roof of the cabin, directly above the table, Pixel built a crude platform for his video camera. He got the idea from birds he saw building nests in trees close to the cabin. He collected twigs from the forest, cut them to size, and by the time the family arrived, his crude platform was ready.

After supper, when Adam started reading to Sally, Pixel lay face down on the platform, and carefully focused the video camera on the pages of *Robinson Crusoe*. With the flickering candle, and Adam's boisterous reading habits, it was not easy for Pixel to get a clear picture of each page, but it was the best he could do.

When Sally went to bed, and Adam read silently, a weary Pixel returned to the spacecraft. He was very satisfied with himself. He had a video of the giants' written language, and an audio of the words being read. It might take time but he was sure that the linguists on Larth would one day be able to decipher the earthlings' language. But he was still not satisfied with the video images.

The next day he waited in his nest in the roof until the family went to work in the fields. They were clearing new ground so that they could plant more corn and wheat.

When he was quite sure that the family was a safe distance away from the cabin Pixel flew to the kitchen table and landed beside *Robinson Crusoe*. He walked on the table to the front of the book, reached up to hold the cover of the book with one hand, and, controlling the anti-gravity switch with his other hand, gently pushed the cover of the book over, so that the front page of the book was open. He then flew directly over the front page, and, in hover mode, videoed the page. After he videoed each page he would fly quickly to the doorway to be sure that the giants were not nearby.

He had videoed about forty pages when he saw Sally running towards the cabin. He flew quickly to the table, grasped the open book cover, and, with a quick burst of engine power, closed the book. He had excellent digital images of the pages. The linguists would be able listen to Adam reading the words, and they would be able to match what he read aloud to the words in the book.

Within a few days he had videoed all the pages in *Robinson Crusoe*. For several weeks he spent hours every night trying to decipher the language. He was very proud when he figured out the numbering system from the page numbers in *Robinson Crusoe*. When Adam started giving Sally lessons in arithmetic, and she wrote "2 + 4 = 6" on her slate, Pixel knew for sure that he had mastered the earthlings' numbering system.

While visiting nearby farms Pixel learned that some humans used four legged creatures to help with the work. He found it strange that living creatures were held captive by humans. On Larth solar powered robots were used for tedious work, wild animals were not domesticated. Pixel wondered why his giant family preferred to do the farm work without using the domesticated creatures.

Adam's main chore in the evenings was chopping wood for the fire, while Sally fed the chickens and Mary cooked supper. One evening, from a tree near the wood pile, Pixel watched the children. Sally loved to tease her brother and Adam would often have to drop his axe and chase his sister around the cabin. Pixel enjoyed watching them play.

PIXEL

Adam was resting on his axe when a noisy cluster of sparrows landed on the branches near to Pixel. Adam immediately dropped the axe and drew his slingshot from his back pocket. He aimed carefully at the birds and shot a stone directly at them. Pixel had no knowledge of slingshots. He did not see the stone racing towards him. The frightened birds took flight when they heard the stone crashing through the leaves. Pixel activated the anti-gravity emergency button, but it was too late. The stone struck his power pack and Pixel was sent tumbling through the branches of the tree.

"Sally, I shot a bird," yelled an excited Adam, as he ran towards the tree.

"It's a green leprechaun," shouted Adam when he saw Pixel desperately hanging on to a leaf. "Come quickly Sally. You must see this."

Adam could see that Pixel was in danger of falling from the leaf. He held out his open hand under Pixel to prevent him from falling to the ground. Pixel released his hold on the leaf and slid into Adam's hand. Pixel tried his anti-gravity switch again, but it was futile. He could not fly.

"Oh my!" exclaimed Sally, when she saw Pixel standing in Adam's hand. "He has a broken wing. We must show this to mother." She ran into the cabin shouting, "A little green man! A little green man!"

Adam cupped his hands and carried Pixel gingerly up the cabin steps and placed him gently on the kitchen table.

"Goodness gracious!' said Mary. "A leprechaun? Where did you find him?"

"I shot him with my slingshot. I was aiming for a sparrow. Do you really think he is a leprechaun?"

"I don't know," said Mary. "I never believed in leprechauns. It's just an Irish faerie story. I never thought that leprechauns really existed."

"He could be a faerie," said Sally. "Can you see his wings? They look broken."

"Perhaps I can fix them," said Adam as he reached over to touch Pixel.

"Adam. Sally. Robinson Crusoe!" Pixel shouted passionately as he rolled under the edge of a plate to avoid Adam's fingers.

"He knows our names," said Sally. "We can talk to him."

"My name is Adam," said Adam, pointing to himself.

"My name is Sally," said Sally pointing to herself.

Pixel rolled out from under the plate, pointed to himself, and shouted, "My name is Pixel."

"Hello, Mr. Pixel," said Sally. "Are you a leprechaun?"

"My name is Pixel," said Pixel.

"Sally, I don't think that he understands English," said Mary. "Let me ask him some questions."

"My name is Mary," said Mary pointing to herself. "Where do you come from, Pixel?"

"My name is Pixel," said Pixel.

"Your name is Pixel," said Mary, pointing at Pixel.

"Your name is Mary," said Pixel, pointing at Mary.

"This is a plate," said Mary, pointing at a plate.

"This is a plate," said Pixel, pointing at the plate.

"Are you a leprechaun?" Mary asked.

"This is a plate," Pixel replied.

"He does not understand English, but he certainly wants to learn," said Mary. "He seems to be quite intelligent. While I'm making supper try to teach him as many words as you can. We'll have to decide, after supper, what we can do to help him."

Sally offered food to Pixel during supper. She cut a grain of corn into small pieces and served it to Pixel in a teaspoon. But Pixel did not eat the corn. He did drink some of the water that was served in another teaspoon. Adam and Sally taught him many words—cup, knife, candle, saucer, table, chair . . . .

Mary wondered what should be done with the little man. She didn't believe in faeries, so she was quite sure that he was not a leprechaun. Where did he come from?

"I think we should set Pixel free," Mary suggested to the children, after supper." He may not be able to eat the food that we eat. He may have friends who can help him. They may be looking for him right now. Adam, what do you think?"

"I would like to keep him for at least one night, mother. He is trying to fix his wing. Maybe he can get it working tomorrow. If we put him outside tonight he could be attacked by field mice, or owls, or anything," Adam replied.

"How do you think he learned about *Robinson Crusoe*, mother?" Sally asked.

"That's a good question Sally," said her mother. "Perhaps he has been watching us."

"So he may have a home nearby?' asked Sally. "He might," said Adam. "But he has wings to fly, so he could live anywhere. Mother, I would just like to keep him for one night. I could build a tree house for him in the morning and he would be free to go whenever he is ready."

"Just for one night, Adam. I want you to set him free in the morning."

Adam and Sally made a bed for Pixel of cloth and feathers. They placed the bed in the bottom of a chest drawer, along with water in a teaspoon. Getting Pixel into the drawer proved to be quite difficult. He would run to the far side of the kitchen table whenever Adam tried to pick him up.

"Be very careful, Adam," said Sally, tearfully, when she saw Pixel running away from Adam. "He's afraid of you."

Eventually Mary and Sally used a rolled up tablecloth to gently push Pixel to the edge of the kitchen table onto a book held by Adam. Pixel was then lowered, on the book, to the bottom of the drawer. He was not happy, but at least he had not been manhandled by Adam. He could not understand why he had been imprisoned. He had enjoyed his language lesson with the family. They seemed to like him. He felt that they recognized him as an intelligent being. He was devastated when he was thrown into a dungeon.

"We are just trying to protect you, Pixel," said Adam, looking down at him in the drawer. "You will be free tomorrow."

There was no response from Pixel. He just stared angrily at Adam.

Sally was in tears. "Please forgive us Pixel," she cried. "We just want to help you."

It was no use. Pixel refused to say another word to the family.

At bedtime Adam carried the wooden drawer up the ladder to the sleeping area, and placed it close to the wall. He whispered goodnight to Pixel. Sally crawled over Adam to look into the darkened drawer. "Be brave Pixel," she murmured. "You will be free in the morning."

Pixel was mortified, and afraid. Despite his technical superiority he was a prisoner of the giants. It was very dark in the drawer but he could see faint rays of moonlight flickering through the cabin wall. When he was quite sure that the family was asleep he removed a solar powered cutting device from his backpack. He cut a hole in the side of the drawer and crawled onto the blanket towards the edge of the bed. The cabin doorway was etched in moonlight. He could see Adam's head just beside the drawer; he was sleeping peacefully. Pixel inched past Adam towards the top of the ladder. The first rung was just a few inches from the edge of the bed, an easy jump for Pixel. The second rung was much further away. Pixel hesitated, he thought that Adam was stirring. He jumped to the second rung and, without stopping, jumped from rung to rung until he was on the cabin floor. He ran quickly to the cabin door and squeezed through a crack at the door jamb. He radioed the spacecraft as he ran towards the wood pile. Had he awakened Adam? Fearfully, he awaited the spacecraft.

When the spacecraft hovered into view Pixel directed it to the far side of the cabin. From the wood pile he ran to the parked spacecraft. He was free!

NEW ORLEANS

Wind powered vessels were unknown on Larth so Pixel was fascinated with the sailing ships in the harbour of New Orleans. During his first week in the tropical city he spent days trying to understand how the giants used wind to power their ships.

Pixel still had painful memories of his imprisonment by the giants. When he escaped from the cabin he had set the spacecraft on autopilot and headed south; he needed sleep to recover from his ordeal. Finding New Orleans was good therapy for Pixel.

In the bustling city he explored storage sheds filled with food, fabrics, building supplies, and tools of all kind. He hovered in smoky saloons, fancy hotels, expensive houses with large libraries, and stables with dozens of horses. He learned that even in the largest cities the giants had not developed the science of using solar power for energy. From a chandelier in a theatre he enjoyed musical plays, and the pleasure and excitement of the giants in the audience. He watched sailors staggering drunkenly back to their ships.

One day Pixel rode aboard a cargo boat as it sailed from the harbour to the open sea. From his position in the highest mast he watched the sailors trimming sails to catch the most favourable winds. When the ship was clear of the harbour and was on a steady course, Pixel flew down to the ship's rudder. Intuitively he understood that the rudder made sailing possible, he wanted to learn how rudders worked. He was examining the rudder when he heard two explosions. The captain started shouting frenzied instructions. Some sailors, armed with swords, ran to the side of the ship. Others were frantically adjusting the sails. Two pirate ships were sailing rapidly towards the cargo boat. The pirates fired two more warning shots. Pixel could see one of the cannon shots fly past the rudder. He flew to a mast to get a better view. Another cannon shot! Pixel felt the rigging on the mast collapse around him. He rocketed out to sea to escape the sails hurtling towards him.

Hovering above the action Pixel could see the lighter, faster pirate ships closing quickly on the cargo ship. Another round of cannon shots crashed into the cargo ship's rigging. The white flag of surrender was raised and the pirates, waving guns and swords, leaped onto the deck of the captured ship.

Pixel followed the pirates as they sailed with their loot towards the mangrove forests that bordered New Orleans. At their secret lair, an island in the swamp, they ate roasted wild pig and drank rum in a wild spree.

Pixel was perplexed by the behaviour of the pirates. There was no violence of any kind on Larth so Pixel could not understand the reason for violence between humans. To know humans he had to learn their language. Perhaps he should return to Mary and the children and resume his lessons. Adam had saved his life. Had they imprisoned him for his own safety? Pixel decided to fly back to the cabin; he missed the family.

It was late summer when Pixel returned to the cabin. The family was busy reaping corn and vegetables to be stored for the winter. Pixel resumed his evening visits, listening and recording, but still wary of making direct contact.

On a warm fall afternoon, when they had finished their chores for the day, Adam and Sally begged their mother to let them go to the river, a mile from their cabin. Adam assured his mother that they would not get close to the river's edge. Adam was a good swimmer, but Sally was still learning.

Pixel followed them through the woods and watched them explore the river bank. They were surprised to find a large canoe hidden in bushes by the sandy bank of the river. They could not imagine who might have hidden the canoe. There were no other cabins close to the river; the family lived on the outskirts of the settlement and the far side of the river was unsettled forests. Adam and Sally crawled under the bushes to get a better look at the inside of the canoe. They were startled when three men rushed from the forest. Two of the men seized Adam and Sally, while the third man quickly launched the canoe into the swiftly flowing river. Adam and Sally were thrown into the canoe, as the two men leapt on board and paddled quickly downstream.

Pixel was terrified. He followed the canoe as it raced down the river. The children held each other tightly as the canoe danced crazily over the waves. After several hours the canoe was beached on the far side of the river and the children were taken to a small encampment in the forest. Pixel saw two tents and several horses. The men were greeted by a woman who was clearly very angry with them. What Pixel did not know was that the woman and the men were people from a different tribe than his giant family. The concept of "tribe" was unknown on Larth. The people of Larth had lived in a form of world government for thousands of years.

The men were three brothers, and the woman was the wife of the oldest brother. Their tribe was part of the nation of people that were the first inhabitants of the continent. They had been driven from their hunting grounds by the European settlers, like Pixel's giants, who were setting up farms in the uncleared forests.

The woman was angry with her husband and his brothers for kidnapping the children. The three men had been looking for her daughter who had been seized several years ago in a skirmish between the native Americans and the colonists. The three brothers had made a rash mistake in taking Adam and Sally. The woman comforted Sally as best she could. She had learned to speak English from members of her tribe who had once traded peacefully with the colonists. She was able to assure Adam and Sally that they would not be harmed, as she led them into the largest tent. Pixel noticed that there was a small opening at the top of the tent and he was able to observe what happened inside the tent. The woman fed the children some soup and encouraged them to rest on a bed of furs in a corner of the tent. She gave them warm clothes, and did everything she could to make them feel safe. Watching this, Pixel realized that he had to return to the cabin. He could not imagine what Mary would do when she discovered that Sally and Adam were missing.

MARY

Mary was worried about the coming winter. It would be her second winter without her husband. There was no word from him, and she had no way of finding out where he might be. The children had worked hard on the farm, but the harvest had not been good. If it was a long winter there might not be enough food for the family.

When the children begged to go to the river she knew that they needed a break from their chores. She trusted her son's good judgement. He was now thirteen years old, and Mary was very proud of his strength and maturity. She was glad to let them have an adventure.

But she became very worried at suppertime when the children had not returned from the river. She hurried to the river and saw the children's footprints on the river bank. Frantically, she scrambled through the bushes alongside the river, desperately hoping that the children had been thrown back to shore. She was now sure that somehow the children had both been carried away by the river. After miles of fruitless searching she knew it was hopeless. She had lost her children.

It was very dark when she finally returned to the cabin. Exhausted, she curled up on the floor, moaning hopelessly with grief.

And that is how Pixel found her. He had to help her. He flew to the spacecraft for a video device that could project images. He had made videos of the children being comforted in the tent. He would show those images to Mary.

He set up the video machine on the edge of the bunk bed and started projecting all the images he had recorded that day. He magnified the images so that they were about the size of a postage stamp when they were projected on the cabin wall. Then he flew down to Mary lying on the floor and shouted in her ears as loudly as he could, "Mary! Mary!"

The room was quite dark and Mary was startled when she looked up to see a tiny creature hovering like a humming bird only inches from her face. And she saw a flickering light on the cabin wall.

"Mary. Mary" shouted Pixel.

Mary was now on her feet. "Pixel?" she said. "Is that you Pixel?"

Pixel flew to the images that were being projected on the cabin wall. He pointed at them. Mary was amazed. She saw tiny moving pictures of Adam and Sally in the tent. They were wrapped in furs, and carefully drinking a broth given to them by an Indian squaw.

"I'm dreaming," said Mary, bewilderedly. "What kind of magic is this?"

Pixel projected the images over and over again. Mary tried touching her children and found the images projected on her fingers.

Finally Pixel froze the projector so that just one image of the children was projected on the wall. It showed Adam and Sally sleeping soundly in the tent.

Mary started to cry, uncontrollably. "Dear God, please tell me this is just a dream. Pixel, why have you cast a spell on my children? We meant you no harm."

Pixel could not understand anything that Mary was saying. He knew she was perplexed so he flew to the table and stood there hoping she would realize that he wanted to help.

"What do you want from me, Pixel?" she said angrily. "What have you done to Sally and Adam?" She lurched forward to try to hold him. Pixel elude her and flew immediately to the projection on the wall. "Adam! Sally!" he shouted, frustratingly, pointing to the children.

Mary started crying again. Perhaps this was just a dream. Perhaps she was losing her mind.

Pixel was on the table again. And this time he walked purposefully to a spoon and pushed it off the table. Mary was startled. She lit a candle and picked the spoon up off the floor. She placed the spoon in the middle of the table and this time, with some effort, Pixel dragged the spoon to the edge of the table and pushed it over again. Mary picked up the spoon once more. "What do you want Pixel? Please bring back Sally and Adam."

Pixel felt that it was pointless to carry on. At least Mary was no longer crying, perhaps he had given her hope. It had been an exhausting day. He was very tired and knew that Mary needed sleep. He hovered directly in front of Mary and said, as positively as he could, "Good night, Mary."

"Good night, Pixel," said Mary. There was nothing else for her to say.

RECONCILIATION

Pixel was awake before dawn. He was not sure how he could help Mary. Perhaps he had made a huge mistake in becoming involved. He wished he could talk directly to his Dad at Mission Control and ask for his advice. That was impossible, Pixel was truly alone. By making contact with the giants he knew that he was endangering the mission. He was compelled to help Mary; he wanted to be friends again.

He crawled through a crack in the roof and saw that Mary was sleeping fitfully in the bunk bed. She had agonized for hours over the images she had seen of Sally and Adam. They were alive, but trapped in a leprechaun's spell. The family had offended Pixel and now he was punishing Mary. She did not believe in leprechauns, they were just old wives' tales. It was too fantastic to be true. But Pixel was real, and he had control of Sally and Adam. When the candle flickered out she had climbed the ladder to the bunk bed and slipped into a troubled sleep.

Pixel decided not to wake her. Instead he returned to the spacecraft and flew to the Indian camp. At high speed the spacecraft was at the camp within ten minutes. The sun was just rising and the children and their captors were still asleep in the tents. He flew back to the cabin and landed the spacecraft on the ground right in front of the chicken coop. The door to the cabin was closed so Pixel had to fly to the roof to get inside. Mary was still asleep. Pixel hovered in front of her face shouting as loud as he could, "Help Sally, Help Adam."

Mary sat up quickly. "Help? What do you mean, Pixel?" she asked, angrily.

Pixel pointed to the door of the cabin shouting, "Sally, Adam, Sally, Adam."

Mary rushed down the ladder and pushed open the cabin door, thinking that Pixel had somehow brought her children home. But when she opened the door all she could see was a strange looking object, about as big as a large melon, on the ground in front of the chicken coop.

Pixel flew to the cigar shaped metal object, opened a tiny door, and went inside. Mary was amazed to see the metal object rise slowly in the air and circle the cabin before landing exactly where it had started. Pixel then walked out of the flying machine and hovered in front of her shouting, "Help Sally, Help Adam," while pointing energetically towards the river. Suddenly he flew into the cabin, and Mary followed him inside. He was now pointing at bread she had baked a few days ago and shouting, "Sally, Adam." It seemed to Mary that the little man wanted her to take food to Sally and Adam. So she wrapped the bread in a towel and followed Pixel as he flew out of the cabin. He immediately got into the spacecraft and headed towards the river. Mary followed the spacecraft as it flew through the forest.

Pixel had programmed the spacecraft to head towards the children, but he had to control the spacecraft manually to avoid trees in the forest. The spacecraft had cameras that viewed outside images and projected the images to multiple television screens that Pixel could watch as he flew. He could keep track of Mary walking quickly behind him, and at the same time be looking ahead for unknown creatures. Pixel hoped that they would get to the children before nightfall. He had no idea what they would do when they got there. He had decided to use the spacecraft because it might be useful if there was conflict with the captors, or if Mary was attacked by wild animals. He had seen animals in the forest that were larger than the giants and he did not know whether or not they might be a threat to Mary. The spacecraft had been designed to deal with unknown threats from life forms the scientists had imagined that Pixel might encounter, but the scientists had not considered giant sized animals.

Mary was thinking only of her children. She had to believe that Pixel, in his magical machine, would lead her to Adam and Sally. But as she walked she also thought how strange it was that she was following a leprechaun in a flying machine! As a young girl she had heard stories of faeries called leprechauns. In those stories the leprechauns were always trying to trick people. But she was too practical to believe in faeries, so who was this little man?

After two hours of walking Mary realized that she was quite hungry. She had not eaten since noon the previous day. She waved at the

PIXEL

spacecraft, and walked to the river which was just a few yards from their route through the forest. She scooped handfuls of water from the river and then ate some of the bread that Pixel had suggested she bring on the trip. "Clever little man," she thought.

Pixel landed the spacecraft on the river bank. He walked out of the tiny cabin door and hovered close to Mary's face.

"You help Sally and Adam?" asked Mary.

"Help Sally and Adam," Pixel replied.

"I help Sally and Adam," said Mary as she pointed to herself.

"I help Sally and Adam," said Pixel as he pointed to himself.

"We help Sally and Adam," said Mary as she pointed to Pixel and to herself.

"We help Sally and Adam," said Pixel as he pointed to Mary and to himself.

"We go now," said Mary as she stood up and pointed down the river.

"We go now," said Pixel.

Pixel sensed a change in Mary's mood. She seemed confident and trusting. Perhaps they could be friends again.

Mary strode through the forest as quickly as possible, confident that that she would soon be with her children. She stopped again late in the afternoon for more water and bread. Pixel estimated that they would reach the children before nightfall. He was starting to doubt his decision to lead Mary on this quest. What would happen when they arrived at the

35

Indian's camp? He had seen giants fighting in New Orleans and knew that they could be very violent. But Mary was on her feet, and ready to go, so Pixel led her further into the forest.

Suddenly the onboard computer warned him of a large life form directly ahead. A hulking black bear stood directly in their path. Pixel immediately turned the spacecraft around to lead Mary away from the bear. But Mary had already seen the bear. She knew about bears. She was not going to let a bear stop her from finding her children. She picked up a large stick and held it high above her head to make herself look as big as possible. "Go away, go away," she said firmly. The bear looked quizzically at Mary, until he was distracted by the spacecraft hovering above him. He lashed out at the spacecraft as it circled, emergency lights flashing on and off, just out of his reach. Frustrated and bemused the bear ran into the underbrush.

Pixel was amazed at Mary's bravery, she was more resourceful than he had imagined. He quickly headed the spacecraft in the direction of the children, and Mary followed, with increased energy.

It was early evening when Pixel realized that they were quite close to the Indian camp. He thought of speeding ahead to learn what was happening at the Indian camp but was concerned that this might be confusing to Mary. So he reduced speed so that Mary had to walk slowly to avoid getting ahead of the spacecraft. Mary realized that they must be getting close to the children so she tread quietly after the flying machine.

Life form detectors on the spacecraft indicated activity ahead, at the same time that Mary heard sounds from the Indian camp. She wanted to be careful, but instead she rushed quickly towards the sounds. Within moments she was in an open area of the forest, with a clear view of Adam and Sally sitting by a fire with four native Americans.

She ran towards them shouting, "Sally, Adam." The children were on their feet immediately and ran towards Mary. The Indian men, who had heard Mary scrambling through the brush, had rushed to their tent to get their rifles. The Indian mother angrily told the men to put the rifles away. She watched Mary and the children, hugging and crying with joy.

The Indian mother walked towards Mary with her arms outstretched, in a sign of peace. "I am glad you have come," she said.

Mary was silent.

"She was very kind to us," said Sally.

"She was trying to get her brothers to take us home," Adam explained.

The Indian mother told Mary how her own daughter had been taken by colonists three years ago. Her daughter would be 12 years old now. She explained to Mary that she had begged her husband to try and find her daughter. Her husband and his brothers had been canoeing up the river for many weeks, stopping and exploring inland whenever they were close to settlements of colonists. Mary's cabin had been their final stop. They realized that with so many new settlements they would not be able to find the colonists who had kidnapped the daughter. The settlement they were looking for was perhaps much further north. They were angry and frustrated when they returned to their canoes. They seized Adam and Sally because they thought it would it would make the Indian mother happy. She told Mary she was very angry with them. She wanted them to take Adam and Sally back to their mother, but her husband and his brothers were afraid that colonists would be looking for them.

She asked Mary if she would stay for the night. She offered food and drink.

"I think we should stay," said Adam. "We trust her, she has been good to us."

Mary was already thinking that it would be very difficult to reach the cabin in the dark. She believed that the Indian mother was sincere. The magical images that Pixel had projected on the wall of the cabin had shown this Indian mother caring for Adam and Sally. The pictures were real. It was not a dream, or a magic spell. And the children trusted the Indian mother.

"Could I have some water?" Mary asked.

The Indian mother led Mary to the fire and gave her a herbal drink. She could see that Mary was very tired. She offered Mary some dried meat and fruit.

"You can sleep in my tent this evening. I will sleep with my husband and his brothers."

Mary was very tired, and very relieved, and very, very happy. "Thank you," she said. "We will stay. But we will be leaving very early in the morning."

The Indian mother took Mary and the children into the tent. The children led her to the sleeping area, and the family laid together in the warmth of the furs.

"How did you find us?" asked Adam.

Mary thought of the little man. "Pixel is back." she said. "He led me to you, in a flying carriage."

"Pixel? In a flying carriage?" Adam exclaimed.

"Is his wing better?" Sally asked.

'I will tell you the story tomorrow. We have a long walk home. Good night, my darlings."

HOME

Sally and Adam were sleeping soundly when Mary awoke the next morning. She was anxious to start the long walk home but she felt they were too content to be disturbed. When she crawled out of the tent she saw the Indian mother and her husband sitting by a fire. The other tent was gone, the two brothers had left early with one of the canoes.

The Indian mother welcomed her. "Please join us for food. I have gifts for Sally and Adam." She gave Mary moccasins for the children to wear home.

Mary sat by the fire. She told the Indian mother that to her knowledge there were no captive Indian children in their community. She thanked her for being a good mother to Sally and Adam. She told the Indian mother that she prayed that there would be peace between their tribes.

There was no sign of Pixel. Mary woke the children and they were given warm food by the Indian mother. When Mary said it was time to leave Adam and Sally hugged the Indian mother and shook hands with the husband.

As soon as the family started the long trek home Mary realized that she did not really know the way. Pixel had led her across the river at a point where it widened and was quite shallow. From that point Pixel had led her away from the river and directly to the children. Without the river as a guide Mary was lost in the forest. She headed north with the rising sun as a guide and hoped that Pixel would return.

"Please tell us about Pixel," Sally asked. "I hope we can see him again."

"And the flying carriage. What did it look like?" asked Adam.

"I have a feeling that we will see him again with his flying carriage," said Mary. "He flew into the cabin last night and showed me tiny images of you sleeping in the tent. I thought he had cast a spell on both of you."

"Tiny images?" asked Adam. "What does that mean?"

"It's hard to explain, Adam. Images of you and Sally appeared on the wall of the cabin. When I tried to touch the images they moved to my finger."

"Did he talk to you?" asked Sally.

"He only said that he wanted to help. He kept repeating your names. Yesterday he woke me up and showed me his carriage. It was right outside the cabin door. He walked into his carriage, through a tiny door, and the carriage rose in the air."

"Like a balloon?" asked Adam

"What did the carriage look like?" asked Sally. "Did it have tiny horses?"

Before Mary could answer the spacecraft hovered into view. "There it is now! Pixel's carriage," said Mary, happily. The children watched in amazement as the spacecraft landed a few yards in front of them, and Pixel appeared. He hovered in front of the awestruck children and said, "Pixel help Sally and Adam."

"Welcome back, Pixel," Sally was leaping with joy. "I am so happy to see you again. Your wings are beautiful."

"Please forgive me, Pixel," said Adam. "I am very sorry that I made you a prisoner."

"Pixel help Sally and Adam," said Pixel.

"I," said Mary slowly, pointing at herself. "I thank you, Pixel."

"I thank you, Mary," Pixel replied.

"We go now, Pixel," said Mary, pointing north.

"We go now, Mary," said Pixel. In minutes the spacecraft was airborne; and Pixel was leading the family home.

The children had endless questions for their mother as they trudged through the forest. Where did Pixel come from? Why was he helping them? Was he from a desert island, like Robinson Crusoe's ? Had he been blown away from his island home?

"I can't imagine where he is from or why he is helping us," said Mary, finally. "It seems that he wants to learn our language; we should teach him."

When they stopped for a rest Pixel left the spacecraft and joined them on the riverbank. "I thank you Mary, Sally, Adam," he said.

Adam had been thinking how to teach Pixel. He picked a leaf from a tree and held it in front of Pixel, "This is a leaf."

Pixel flew to the leaf, touched it, and said, "This is a leaf."

Sally picked up a stone and said, "This is a stone," and of course Pixel replied, "This is a stone."

The children continued the game with "tree", "dirt", "branch", "ant', "flower", and just about everything they could see around them. Pixel was delighted with the game.

Finally Mary stood up, pointed north and said, "Pixel, please lead us home." Pixel understood and immediately resumed the flight to the cabin.

At their next rest stop Sally and Adam taught Pixel more words, 'water', 'drink water', 'pour water', 'river', 'riverbank', 'bird', 'sky'. And at every rest stop they added new words. They also tested Pixel with old words. Adam held up a leaf and said, 'Pixel what is this?' And Pixel replied, "This is a leaf." He caught on quickly and his answers were mostly correct.

This learning game made the trek home great fun for the children, but Mary worried that they were spending too much time at each rest stop. There were many miles to travel and, as Mary had feared, by nightfall they were still many miles from home. It was too dark to go further so she stopped and waved to Pixel to turn around. Pixel immediately understood the problem and he turned on the flood lights on the underside of the spacecraft. As soon as Mary saw the lights she knew that they could carry on. So she waved Pixel on. Pixel made sure the spacecraft stayed close to the family so that they could get the maximum benefit from the lights.

Within an hour they were home, and Pixel had a creative idea. He had observed that Mary lit the candle each evening from flames in the fireplace. He had noticed that, if there was no fire in the fireplace, she had to use a tinder box to light the candles. The tinder box was a small metal box which contained charred cloth and small pieces of very dry wood. Mary rubbed together two pencil like pieces of steel and flint to create a spark in the tinder box. The spark caused the charred cloth to flame and that started the dry wood burning. Mary could then light the candle from the burning wood. It was a very slow process and Mary avoided this by keeping a small fire going, every day, in the fireplace. Pixel thought he could help. He landed the spacecraft on the ground in front of the cabin and directed searchlights from the spacecraft to the door of the cabin.

Adam and Sally were delighted.

"We won't need candles tonight," said Adam, happily, as he opened the cabin door and the light from the space craft illuminated the kitchen area.

"Pixel is a great friend," said Sally.

Pixel flew into the well lit cabin and said, "Pixel help?"

"Thank you Pixel," said Adam and Sally in unison.

Mary knew that everyone was tired and needed sleep. So she said to Pixel, "Thank you Pixel, and good night."

Pixel knew exactly what good night meant. "Good night, Mary,' he said and flew out the door. He knew that Mary wanted the family to go to bed. He turned off the spacecraft's outer lights and parked it on top of the chicken coop. He needed sleep too, and there was no need to hide the spacecraft from these giants.

PIXEL'S EDUCATION

Pixel awoke before dawn the next morning, and he could not go back to sleep. His mind was racing with endless possibilities. He was a friend of the giants. They were teaching him their language. They liked him. He liked the family and wanted to help them. He thought of all the special tools he had on the spacecraft that had been designed to help him survive on the planet. Could some of these tools be helpful to this family? Would helping one family create conflict with other families? How could he help this family without other families finding out? Would he be in danger if other families found out about him? He told himself that he could always fly away if there was danger. When he was not in the spacecraft he had programmed it to take flight whenever the motion monitors detected any creature that came too close. If he was careful he would be safe. There was so much to learn.

He also recognized that Mary's family was quite poor relative to other families he had observed. Most had horses to help with hoeing the soil for planting. Mary and Adam hoed the soil without horse power. Most other families had a male and female adult, plus several children, to do the farm work. Mary did not have a husband, perhaps he was dead. Adam and Sally certainly helped, Mary could not have managed without their help. But it was a struggle for her. So Pixel was determined to help. He had lots of ideas but they would have to be tested. Perhaps he should be patient and wait until he learnt the language so that he could discuss his ideas with Mary. But Pixel was not very patient.

Mary was also awake before dawn. There was much to do. The chickens had not been fed for two days so she opened the cabin door and headed for the chicken coop. She laughed when she saw Pixel sitting on the chicken coop in front of his flying carriage!

"Good morning, Pixel," she said cheerfully, as she walked towards the chicken coop.

She owed so much to this little man, she thought. She had been so despondent when it seemed that Sally and Adam had drowned. She feared that her husband might also be dead, drowned in a shipwreck. She was alone. She was not sure what she might have done if Pixel had not magically appeared with his offer of help.

Pixel walked to the edge of the roof of the chicken coop. "Good morning Mary," he said. "Pixel help."

The children had so much fun teaching Pixel new words that Mary thought she should give it a try.

"These are chickens," she said.

"These are chickens," said Pixel.

"Many chickens," said Mary as she waved at the chickens chattering around her as she scattered corn to them. "Many chickens," said Pixel.

Eggs, corn, coop and feed were some of the words Pixel learned before Mary returned to the cabin.

Mary was starting to make the fire so that she could prepare a good breakfast for Adam and Sally. She was trying to get a spark in the tinder box when Pixel flew to the fireplace and said, "Pixel help." He pointed a tiny, pin like object towards the kindling in the fireplace and, to Mary's great surprise, a flame appeared which lit the kindling and soon logs were burning brightly.

"A flame maker!" said a grateful Mary. "Thank you, Pixel."

When the children had been served breakfast Mary wondered whether or not she should offer food to Pixel. She laughed to herself at the thought, would she serve him one grain of corn? But it was good manners to make the offer. She filled a teaspoon with tiny morsels of food from her own plate and pushed the teaspoon towards Pixel. "Food for Pixel?" she asked.

Pixel hesitated for a moment. He had been so busy chatting with Sally and Adam that he did not notice what Mary had cooked. Since all Larthans were vegetarian it would be best to avoid Mary's food. He wanted to explain this to Mary without offending her.

Adam noticed Pixel's dilemma. He realized that Pixel did not know the words 'yes' and 'no'.

"Look, Pixel," said Adam, pushing his own plate towards the center of the table. "No, thank you." He pulled the plate towards himself and said.

48

"Yes, thank you." Adam repeated the steps several times before Pixel understood.

"No thank you," said Pixel, pushing the teaspoon of food to Mary.

Mary was beginning to realize that teaching Pixel English was going to take time. She and the children were going to be very busy harvesting corn, potatoes and other vegetables; food to be stored for the long winter which was just weeks away. She had to share her concerns with the children.

"Children," she began. "We need to talk about Pixel. He really wants to help us. I don't know why he wants to help and how long he will stay. He has magical tricks in his flying carriage that he wants to share with us. He started the fire this morning with a magic flame maker. I think we can learn a lot from him. He wants us to teach him English. I want to help him, but we have to harvest the crops for winter. I am worried that he will take too much of your time."

"What do you want us to do?" asked Adam.

"Just work very hard on your chores during the day," said Mary. "In the evening we can take turns teaching him English."

"Should we just ignore him all day?" asked Sally. "He might fly away."

"Pixel is very clever, Sally," her mother answered. "I am sure he will understand that we have work to do. You can talk to him while you are doing your chores."

Pixel must have understood because for most of the day he just watched the family working and avoided getting close enough for a discussion. He studied other farms nearby. He also spent time in the spacecraft putting his ideas on a computer program.

When the family stopped working for the day, and Mary was making supper, Pixel demonstrated his "flame maker" to Adam and Sally by lighting a candle. Adam and Sally taught him the names of every article in the cabin. Blanket, knife, spoon, table, and so on.

After supper Pixel showed videos to the family. He had Mary and Adam move the kitchen table to the far end of the cabin. When he projected videos from the kitchen table to the opposite wall the images were the size of the Robinson Crusoe book that Adam had read.

Adam and Sally were awed when they saw videos of themselves with the Indian mother. Mary told them that these were the images that gave her hope that they were still alive. Pixel then showed them videos that he thought would be the most impressive—pictures of earth as seen from the spacecraft during the orbiting phase. The children had never been to school so they did not know what the images represented. Mary had seen maps of the world in Boston. She explained to the children that they were looking at pictures of Earth, the planet they lived on. Images that perhaps no one else on Earth had ever seen. Pixel showed an image of North America to see if Mary could recognize what she saw. "There's Boston," she said. "Your father and I lived there before we moved to this cabin."

She traced a line on the video map on the wall far inland from Boston. "Our cabin is somewhere in the this area," she said.

Pixel then showed them a series of pictures of North America. The first picture showed an area that included Boston. Each successive picture showed a smaller area as the video camera got closer to earth. The final picture showed the cabin with Mary, Adam and Sally working on the farm.

"That is amazing Pixel," said Mary. "Quite amazing!" She explained to the children that there were several planets that circled the sun, and that Earth was just one of those planets. She knew the names of two other planets—Venus and Mars.

"Can we see Venus and Mars?" asked Adam.

"Let's go outside and look," said Mary.

It was a cloudless night, perfect for star gazing.

"There," said Mary, pointing to one of the brightest stars, "there is Venus."

The children were very thoughtful.

"Do you think that Pixel came from Venus?" asked Sally.

"Or perhaps one of the other planets?" asked Adam.

"I think we should ask him," said Mary.

Pixel was pleased with the family's reaction to the videos. He did not understand what they were saying. He wanted to tell them that he was from another planet, but he did not have the words.

"Pixel, this is our home." said Mary pointing to the ground at her feet. "Mary's home. Adam's home. Sally's home."

She pointed to Venus. "Pixel's home?" she asked.

"No," said Pixel. He pointed to another part of the night sky, "This is Pixel's home."

This was a fantastic idea. Beyond Mary's comprehension. Now she wanted more than ever to hear Pixel's story. Teaching Pixel English was going to be very rewarding.

"Welcome to Earth! We help Pixel," said Mary.

SPRING

—◆—

It had been a challenging but rewarding winter for Pixel. The major challenge was snow. The first winter storm of the year threatened to engulf the parked spacecraft. Pixel had to flee south. When he returned, after the storm subsided, the cabin and the chicken coop were blanketed with snow. Pixel circled the cabin, looking for a place to land. Suddenly Adam ran from the cabin and directed Pixel to the woodpile. Adam had created a landing pad for the spacecraft. Using chopped firewood he had built a crude, flat topped table. Pixel was able to land on the snow free firewood table. Adam ensured that it was snow free for the rest of the winter.

There were many rewards. Pixel could now speak and understand basic English. The family learned more about their own country from the videos Pixel showed them of Boston, New York, and other cities that he had visited. Mary had taught him some Earth history, and the family learned a lot more about Larth. Most rewarding was Pixel's feeling of companionship within the family.

In early spring, when it was warm enough to work outside the cabin, Pixel started testing his chore saving ideas. He had tried to explain his ideas to Mary but she was much too busy to listen. Adam, on the other hand, was very interested in Pixel's proposals. The thought that boring chores could be eliminated was an appealing prospect. Adam became an enthusiastic partner in Pixel's schemes.

"Pixel, I think this stone might work," said Adam. He had lifted a large jagged rock from a pile of stones behind the cabin. It was a heavy stone and Adam struggled to move it to Pixel who was standing on the ground in front of the pile.

"I think so." said Pixel. He was holding a nozzle that was attached to cord like material extending from the spacecraft. Pixel pointed the nozzle at the rock and Adam could see a bright light, a laser beam, cutting into the stone. Within an hour Pixel had bored a hole right through the rock.

"Amazing!" said Adam, when he examined the hole. "I think it's wide enough, Pixel. Should I thread the string through the hole?"

"Yes, Adam," said Pixel. "I don't think the string is strong enough, but we can try."

Adam tied one end of the string to a pebble that was small enough to drop through the hole; he used the pebble to pull the string through the hole. He then knotted the pebble end of the string to the string at the other end of the hole.

"That's good," said Pixel. "I will tie the string to the flying carriage." He pulled a retractable cable from the back of the spacecraft and tied the string to the hook at end of the cable. "Are you ready for the first experiment?"

"I'm ready," Adam replied.

Pixel used his remote control to slowly raise the spacecraft to lift the rock from the ground. Snap! The string broke.

"You were right, Pixel," said Adam. "We will have to use rope instead. But how will we attach the rope to such a little hook? The rope that we have is too thick to pass through the hole in the hook."

"I have an idea, Adam. But you will have to get help from the blacksmith. We need an iron ring, a little smaller than a horseshoe, that we could attach to the hook. The iron ring should be big enough for us to pass the rope through it. What do you think?"

"The blacksmith is a good friend," said Adam. "I'm sure he would help. But he would probably want to know why we need an iron ring. We can't tell him that we have a flying carriage."

"Your mother might know what to do," said Pixel.

Mary did have an idea. She explained to the blacksmith that she wanted the iron ring as part of a pulley for raising and lowering her iron pot from the fireplace.

The iron ring worked. Adam attached it to the hook on the retractable cable, knotted a rope to it, and threaded the rope through the hole in the rock. He then tied the rope off securely with a slip free knot.

With his remote control Pixel raised the spacecraft so that it was about twelve inches off the ground. The spacecraft advanced slowly over the corn field, pulling the jagged rock through the weeds. The rock was heavy enough that it not only dislodged the weeds it also ploughed furrows in the ground where seeds could be planted. When the spacecraft reached the end of the row Pixel turned it around and ploughed another row. He landed the spacecraft and looked at Mary for a reaction. "What do you think, Mary?" he asked.

Mary was astonished. "My goodness," she said. "Pixel, I can't believe that your magic wand is so powerful. I know you are a very clever person, Pixel, but how do you tell the flying carriage what to do?"

"It is not magic, Mary," said Pixel. "Some clever men on Larth designed the flying carriage. They taught me what to do. In the future I am quite sure that your scientists will make clever flying carriages."

Pixel used the spacecraft to plough all the fields on the farm, in just a few days. It saved the family weeks of back breaking work.

Adam found another use for the spacecraft. To maintain a regular supply of fire wood Adam would cut down small trees in the forest and haul them to the wood pile. Adam started using the spacecraft to haul the trees from the forest. It was a simple matter. He tied rope around the trees, attached the rope to the iron ring, and Pixel would direct the spacecraft to pull the tree to the cabin. More work saved.

Sally wanted to know about the food that Pixel ate. He explained to her that he had special tools in his flying carriage that he used to test the leaves, seeds and flowers of the plants that grow wild in the forest.

"Do you make meals from leaves?" Sally asked. "How do you cook your meals in the flying carriage?"

"I have a special box for cooking," said Pixel. "I try a mix of various leaves and flowers to see what tastes best."

"And how do they taste?" Sally asked.

"Not very good," said Pixel, laughing. "Your mother is a much better cook than I am. Your meals smell delicious to me."

Mary gave Sally a small iron pot so that she could cook some of the edible plants that Pixel had tested. Most of Sally's concoctions failed the Pixel/Adam taste test. But Sally was proud of her successes, especially the ones her mother chose for the family's regular meals.

Pixel soon realized that the children thought of the spacecraft as a wonderful toy. Every day after their chores, and before supper, he would show them different features of the spacecraft.

What delighted the children most was the all-terrain vehicle that Mission Control had included in the spacecraft. Pixel had not yet used the vehicle on earth. He found flying a much easier way to explore the planet than driving on land.

For his first demonstration he parked the spacecraft in front of the cabin and then opened the rear door. What the children saw was a tiny door that opened downwards to form a ramp that rested on the ground. When they bent over to look inside the spacecraft, the all-terrain vehicle, with Pixel driving, roared down the ramp! Pixel drove the vehicle at top speed through a hole in the chicken coop fence and startled the chickens! He then circled the yard several times before driving up the ramp and back into the spacecraft.

"Could I have a look at that land carriage?" Adam asked, stooping down to look inside the spacecraft.

"If you can catch it." Pixel replied. He used his remote control to back the all-terrain vehicle down the ramp and drove it at great speed between Adam's legs! Adam fell back in surprise, but was on his feet quickly to chase the land carriage around the cabin. Sally joined the chase. The children shouted gleefully as they ran after the tiny vehicle. If they got too close the land carriage darted under the cabin, behind the chicken coop, or under a thick bush. Mary rushed from the cabin. "What in tarnation!" she exclaimed.

"It's just another carriage, Mary," said Pixel, laughing. He halted the tiny vehicle so that Mary could see it.

"A carriage without a horse," said Sally with a giggle. "Adam and I have been trying to catch it."

"Can we touch it now, Pixel?" Adam asked.

"You can hold it in your hand," Pixel replied. "But please be careful."

Pixel allowed the children to play with the horseless carriage on the kitchen table. The family marvelled as the tiny vehicle weaved its way between cups and plates, and around knives and forks, without ever falling off the table.

Pixel started reading a weekly Boston newspaper. It was Mary's idea. Pixel was asking endless questions about the war between America and Great Britain. The snippets of news that Mary learned from the shopkeeper and the blacksmith were not enough for Pixel. In frustration Mary explained how newspapers were published and sent Pixel on a mission to Boston. He found the building where a newspaper was published and watched the printing process. When the newspapers were stacked for delivery Pixel made a video of the front page. At the cabin he projected the video of the front page on a wall. The words were too tiny for Mary to read but just right for Pixel. He read the news aloud to the family. Mary explained new words and unfamiliar concepts. It became a pleasurable weekly event.

Pixel was on one of his weekly trips to Boston when Adam saw the stranger. He called out to Mary excitedly, "Look Mom, we have a visitor!"

The family watched as a young man on horseback approached the cabin. When he reached them he took off his hat, bowed respectfully to Mary, and asked, "Is your name Mary Lane?"

Mary had never seen this young man before. "Yes, my name is Mary Lane. Do I know you?"

"No," he said, "But I know your husband, Bill Lane. I have a message from him. Can I speak with you?"

Mary shuddered. She held on to Adam to keep from falling. "Bill's alive!" she gasped. "Thank God! Of course, come inside."

"Dad's alive! Dad's alive, Sally!" shouted Adam.

Sally squealed with delight.

"Come inside, please come inside." said Mary, breathlessly.

BILL

Bill was twelve years old when he ran away from an orphanage in Plymouth, a port town on the south coast of England. The people at the orphanage told Bill that his mother had died when he was four, and that his father was a sailor. Bill wanted adventure; he wanted to be free, so he stowed away on a boat that was anchored in Plymouth harbour. The cargo boat was at sea for two days before the cook discovered Bill hiding in the food storage area. The captain of the ship was very angry at first, but when he heard Bill's story he gave Bill a chance to become a sailor by turning him over to the cook and giving him the title "cook's mate".

Bill was very hard working and grew to become a strong, skilled sailor. When his kindly captain retired Bill obtained a position as first mate on a merchant ship trading between England and the North American colonies. He was 22 years old when he met Mary in Boston. His ship had loaded its cargo and was set to sail for Jamaica the following morning. The captain had allowed the crew time off in the afternoon to explore the town. Bill was walking down the main street when he saw a runaway horse heading directly towards a young woman crossing the street. He was only a few yards away, so he ran to her, picked her up in his powerful arms, and put her down safely and gently on the other side of the street.

At that time Mary was living in two small rooms with her ailing mother. Mary had grown up on a farm about fifty miles from Boston. But her father died unexpectedly when he was still a young man. Since there were no sons to take over the farm, Mary's mother sold it and moved to Boston with Mary, her only child.

Realizing that Bill had saved her from serious injury Mary wanted desperately to show her gratitude. When he told her that he was a sailor whose ship was leaving in the morning she invited him to her home for tea and cakes, and to meet her mother. Bill accepted with pleasure.

Although the mother was quite sick she and Mary did everything they could to make Bill's visit a very pleasant one. Bill was entranced. The tender feelings that he saw between mother and daughter made him realize how much he was missing by not having a family of his own. He also realized the love he felt for Mary.

In his long walk back to the ship Bill decided that he must make a life changing decision. It was not unlike the decision he had made when he ran away from the orphanage. Now he wanted to stay in Boston and help Mary care for her mother. He knew that Mary was just being kind to him because he had saved her life. She might be very offended if he offered his help. He also knew that the captain would not allow him to leave the ship in Boston. Bill would not be paid for the voyage until the ship returned to England. There seemed to be no solution to his problems, but he knew that he had to stay in Boston.

By the time he reached the ship he still had not made a decision. As first mate, Bill had a bunk just outside the captain's cabin. He laid in his bunk agonizing over his options. The captain was still ashore. Bill had a key to the captain's cabin. He entered the cabin and opened the captain's safe. He took ten Spanish dollars from the safe. In his mind, this was less than the amount owed to him by the captain. Yet he knew that what he did was wrong. He walked down the gang plank and into the streets of Boston.

The captain would of course send out a search party in the morning when it was discovered that the first mate was missing. Crew members would search the harbour streets in Boston. Knowing this Bill walked all night, away from downtown Boston and into the rustic countryside. He found a place to sleep in woods close to a dairy farm. He was awake by midday and walked back to Boston. On the outskirts of Boston he found an inn with food and shelter for the night.

The next day he walked to Mary's place. She and her mother were very surprised. Bill told them that he was weary of life at sea, and wanted to settle in this new country. Mary had friends in Boston who helped Bill to get a job as a blacksmith's assistant.

Bill moved into a boarding house, close to Mary and her mother. He visited them every evening and helped in any way he could. Often he would just sit with the mother while Mary took a break from the increasing care that her mother needed. He read to her and told her wild stories of his adventures with pirates. They were not always true stories, but they made Mary's mother laugh.

Within three months of Bill's arrival in Boston the mother died.

In those three months Mary learned the real reason that Bill had deserted his ship. He was an orphan trying to find the love he had never received as a child. He was a good man. When Bill asked her to marry him it was easy to say yes.

Like many other young couples they decided to start a farm on the frontier. They joined a horse-drawn wagon train that took colonists to the frontier territories, many miles inland from Boston. After weeks of travel they reached their new home—acres of forested land that had never been cultivated. There was a small brook that flowed through the forest and, close to the brook, Bill and Mary found an open meadow. There they decided to build a new home.

In the summer of their first year they lived in a crude canvas tent. In the winter they built a makeshift lean-to in the forest, with tree brushes and canvas to keep out the snow. By the end of the next summer Bill and Mary had built their log cabin. In the winter of that year, Adam was born, in the new cabin.

In 1775, the year before Pixel landed on Earth, Bill made another life changing decision. He was very proud of what Mary and he had accomplished. They had worked extremely hard to make the farm a success. They grew enough food to last through the winter, the eggs from the chickens could be traded for supplies, and Adam and Sally were happy and healthy. But Bill was restless. He felt that he could expand the farm if he had money to buy a horse and a plough. He had also heard that experienced American sailors were needed in Boston; the British navy was trying to stop American ships from getting much needed supplies from France.

Bill did not realize how dangerous a sea voyage would be until he arrived in Boston and talked to sailors at the port. Every sailor that he met was proud to be helping their country in the war with Great Britain. Bill had no animosity to his own country, Great Britain. But his wife and children were Americans and, now that he had created a home on the American frontier, he felt that he was also an American.

Because of his experience Bill was given the position of first mate on a cargo ship bound for Cuba. When the ship sailed with a strong breeze out of Boston harbour, Bill felt at home again. He wished that his family could be with him to enjoy the salty freshness of the wind and the gentle sound of the waves washing against the ship's bow.

The voyage to Cuba was uneventful. With a full load of sugar the ship crossed the Atlantic ocean and entered the English Channel. This was the most dangerous part of the voyage. British warships patrolled these waters. Bill's captain sailed the ship close to the French shore until it reached Le Havre, a French port that was beyond the reach of British warships. France was also at war with Great Britain and was helping the

Americans by providing them with goods that were not available in the colonies. In fact a shipment of guns was included with other supplies loaded in Bill's ship at Le Havre.

On the return voyage to Boston the ship was met by a fierce storm as it sailed out of the English Channel. The storm drove the ship to the English shore. When the storm subsided the ship was intercepted and seized by a British warship and the guns were discovered in the cargo. A sailor on the British warship recognized Bill. He was one of the sailors who had been sent to search for Bill when he deserted his ship in Boston harbour. The sailor told the captain of the British warship that Bill had stolen ten Spanish dollars when he deserted the ship. The entire American crew was imprisoned on the Isle of Wight, a small island off the southern coast of England. Bill was tried in court as an Englishman who betrayed his country and stole money from his ship. He was found guilty by the court and sentenced to ten years in prison.

THE STRANGER

When Pixel returned from Boston, and saw the horse in front of the cabin, he flew the spacecraft to a special tree in the forest where Adam had built a landing platform. (It was Adam's idea that Pixel should have a place to hide the spacecraft if they ever had visitors.) Pixel then returned to the cabin and entered through the roof. Mary was sobbing quietly and Adam, standing with his arm around her shoulder, said bravely, "We will find a way to free Dad. I know we can find a way. We should go to town tomorrow and talk to the blacksmith. He seems to know a lot about the war. I'm sure he can help us."

"Don't lose heart," said the stranger. "The authorities in Boston know that Bill is a prisoner. They will do what they can to get him released. I told them about you, Mary. They know that he has an American family. I will be returning to Boston in a few weeks time; I will send you a letter when I find out what's happening."

"Thank you, Peter," said Mary. "That is very kind of you. How long will you be staying in Boston?"

"Not long," said Peter. "I am going to join the rebel army. George Washington needs our help."

"I am very proud of you," said Mary, passionately. "I hate war; but I wish you Godspeed. You have given us hope. I thank you with all my heart for bringing us news that Bill is alive and well."

"I should be leaving now." said Peter.

"Please stay for the night," Mary insisted. "It's a long ride home for you. It's the least we can do to thank you for bringing us such good news."

"That is kind of you, Mary. I would be thankful to stay for the night."

Pixel was quite confused by what he had heard. The conversation seemed to be about Mary's husband. She had never talked about him before, and neither had the children, so Pixel had assumed that he was dead. But her husband was alive, and he had to be freed. Pixel did not sleep well that night.

In the morning he waited on the top of the chicken coop until the stranger rode away on his horse. He then flew into the cabin, landed on the kitchen table and asked excitedly, "How can I help? Mary, how can I help?"

Mary looked sadly and affectionately at her little friend. "Thank you Pixel. I wish you could help. But this is more complicated than you could imagine. We are going in to town to see if someone there can help us."

"Please tell me more," asked Pixel, "I only heard a part of the conversation last night."

"Well," said Mary, "the most important thing to know is that Bill is a prisoner of the British navy. He has been charged with treason and will be in prison for ten years. He is being held in a place called the Isle of Wight. The stranger that visited last night, Peter, was a prisoner with Bill. Peter promised Bill that he would bring news to us as soon as he could. Peter has given us the name and address of a friend of his in the Isle of Wight. We can send letters to Peter's friend, who has promised to deliver them to Bill."

"Our dad may one day be sent to Australia by the British," Adam added. "Peter said that he read about this in an English newspaper on the day his ship sailed to America from the Isle of Wight. The British are planning to send their convicts to work for years in Australia."

"Perhaps I could take the message to Peter's friend. Where is the Isle of Wight?" asked Pixel.

"Mom, I think that's a great idea," said Adam, excitedly. "Dad has a map of England. He was born in Plymouth, he showed me where it was on his map. I think the Isle of Wight is nearby. I'll get the map."

Mary had been worrying all night about how she would get to Boston. She had no money for the trip. Perhaps the shopkeeper could sell the farm for her, he might loan her money. She was hoping that the blacksmith might be helpful, he might know of travellers who could take a message to the authorities in Boston. She was anxious to get to town to talk to the blacksmith.

"We can use your help, Pixel," said Mary, hopefully. "But I don't know how you would find the address, there may be thousands of homes on the Isle of Wight."

Adam ran up with the map of England. "Here is Plymouth, Pixel," he said, "And close by is the Isle of Wight."

When Pixel saw on the map that the Isle of Wight was on the south coast of England he said, "I can get there in about six hours."

"Six hours?" Mary was incredulous. "Can you really fly to England in six hours?"

"Yes, Mary," Pixel insisted. "The flying carriage is very fast. I fly it slowly when I am close to the cabin because I do not want to frighten you. I can fly to Europe in just six hours."

"Is there room for a message inside the flying carriage?" asked Adam.

"I think so," said Pixel. "I have an idea. Mary, would you mind if I landed the flying carriage on your table?"

"Can he Mom?" said Adam and Sally, excitedly.

"Goodness gracious!" said Mary. "Pixel, of course you can. Bring your flying carriage inside. I'll clear the table."

Pixel landed the spacecraft right in the middle of the kitchen table, drove the all-terrain vehicle down the ramp, and parked it at the very edge of the table. He made a theatrical bow when he stepped out of the vehicle.

Adam and Sally clapped with delight. Mary just smiled.

Pixel walked over to the rear entrance of the spacecraft, and stood on the ramp. 'If you can fold a paper message that will fit inside the flying carriage, I can deliver it to Peter's friend."

"Can I try, Mom?" asked Sally.

Sally folded a sheet of writing paper in different ways until she found a size that could be inserted through the rear door of the spacecraft. Pixel had rearranged components within the spacecraft to make room for the message. The all-terrain vehicle would be left with Adam who had promised Pixel that he would keep it in a safe place, and would not use it as a toy.

Once Sally had inserted the folded sheet of paper into the spacecraft the next test was for Pixel to try and pull the message out of the spacecraft. This was awkward for Pixel until Sally decided to tie a string around the message to keep it from unfolding inside the spacecraft.

While Sally and Pixel were experimenting with folding messages Mary and Adam were composing the message they thought should be sent. They decided on two messages. The first one said:

Dear Mrs. Blackburn,

Your good friend, Peter Walsh, has told me that you have been kind enough to offer to deliver messages to my husband, Bill Lane. I am very grateful to you for this kindness. I am sure that you understand how worried I am for Bill's safety. This message has been delivered to you by a friend of mine who does not want to be recognized. You may receive more messages in this way.

Please give the attached letter to Bill. If you can meet with Bill please tell him that a gentleman who goes by the name of Pixel may try to meet with him. Please tell Bill that we have great trust in this gentleman.

Thank you so much for your help. My family will always be indebted to you.

Yours sincerely,

Mary Lane

The second message read:

Dear Bill,

Adam and Sally and I are overjoyed to learn that you are alive and well! Peter Walsh brought your message yesterday. I feared that you might have drowned at sea. Adam and Sally are both well. They have been a great help to me. They love and miss you very much. We are going to do all we can to get you released from prison.

We have a good friend who may visit you from time to time. He is a very little man, quite unusual, but very resourceful. His name is Pixel. I trust him.

Your loving wife and children,
Mary, Adam and Sally'

Sally folded both messages and inserted them in the body of the spacecraft. Pixel raised the ramp and closed the rear door of the spacecraft. "I'm ready to go," he said. 'Mary, I'm not sure how long it will take me to find Bill, but I will return with news as soon as possible."

Mary tried to imagine how this little man could possibly deliver a letter to Bill. But her confidence in Pixel was now unbounded.

"Be careful, Pixel," said Mary lovingly, as she reached out to touch his fingers. It was a symbol of affection that Sally had invented.

Pixel reached up to touch Mary's outstretched finger. And then he flew off to his adventure on the Isle of Wight.

ISLE OF WIGHT

Pixel flew over the Atlantic at a high altitude so that the spacecraft could achieve maximum speed. Within four hours he reduced speed and altitude and soon had an overview of Great Britain. The Isle of Wight was easily recognized on the south coast. Pixel also noticed how close the island was to France, a friend of America and an enemy of Great Britain. He still could not understand why the people of Earth should be at war with each other. On Larth, every problem was resolved by discussion and rational thinking. Government, as we know it, does not exist on Larth; all problems were resolved by individuals communicating with each other over the Larthan world wide communication system. It was a system somewhat like the internet, but much more advanced.

There were several small towns on the Isle of Wight, mostly on the coast. The largest town was on the southern tip of the island. Pixel decided that he would begin his search for Mavis Blackburn in this town. He hovered over the town and, using the spacecraft's imaging system, made an overhead video of the town that showed all of the streets. He parked the spacecraft in a tree outside the town and studied the video map of the streets to see if there was a logical pattern that would help him find Seaside Lane. Unfortunately the streets were laid out in a jigsaw fashion so it was not going to be easy. He flew in a series of straight lines, from east to west, checking the name of every street that he crossed. He searched all day but he could not find Seaside Lane. It was getting dark when he realized that this was the wrong town.

The next morning when he flew to the second largest town, on the north coast, he was surprised to see a large number of British warships in the harbour. Perhaps Bill's prison was also in this port.

He found Seaside Lane as soon as he started his search. It was on the most westerly part of the town, and some distance from the docks. The lane ended in a sandy beach, and number 4 was very close to the beach. It was a very quiet lane, but there were fishing boats on the beach with some fishermen tending their nets. Pixel decided that he should deliver the message later that night. He watched the house for most of the day and a white haired lady was the only person that he saw entering or leaving the house. He assumed that she must be Mavis Blackburn.

Just before midnight, he landed the spacecraft on the doorstep of number 4 Seaside Lane. He pulled out the two messages that Sally had inserted in the spacecraft, untied them, and slipped them under the front door. He flew into the house and made sure that the messages were clearly visible in the front hallway. After hiding the spacecraft he returned to the house, and was soon fast asleep under a couch in Mrs. Blackburn's living room.

When she awoke the next morning Mrs. Blackburn had a leisurely breakfast in her kitchen which looked out on her small, rose filled garden. Pixel was getting impatient, he had been up for several hours and was worried that Mrs. Blackburn might want to spend the morning in her rose garden. There was a small brass candlestick on a side table in the living room. Pixel nudged it off the table and the clatter had Mrs Blackburn running into the living room. "Goodness gracious," she said when she saw the candle holder on the floor. And then she saw the two messages.

"My goodness!" she murmured to herself when she had read both messages. She gathered her coat and hat and set off immediately for the Royal Navy prison.

Pixel followed her as she walked up the lane and turned right on to Harbour Street. He soon realized that Harbour Street followed the coastline and that it ended on the far side of town where the British warships were moored. He flew ahead of Mrs. Blackburn to see if he could identify the prison. When he reached the edge of town he saw a large, square building that he was quite sure was the prison. It was situated on a very large property and was enclosed on all sides by high stone walls. Behind the stone wall at the rear of the building was a rocky beach, and a wharf that jutted out into the sea. When he flew into one of the rooms at the rear of the building and saw men sitting or lying on beds of straw he knew that it was a prison cell. The window that he flew through had three iron bars which prevented the prisoners from escaping. It was the only window in the cell.

Pixel flew to the front of the prison to see if there was a way for him to get in without being noticed. He wanted to see Mrs. Blackburn give Mary's message to Bill so that he could recognize him. He might be able to deliver future messages directly to Bill.

He discovered that there were regular windows in the front rooms of the building. These rooms seemed to be offices of some kind. Confident that he could get into the prison easily, Pixel returned to Mrs. Blackburn. The walk to the prison was quite long and Mrs. Blackburn was hot and tired when she arrived at the prison gate.

"Good morning Tom," she said to the guard in the front office of the prison. "Fancy meeting you here. I thought you were still sailing the seven seas." Mrs Blackburn had lived all her life in this small town. She was the widow of a popular sea captain who often had crew members visit him at his cottage. Tom had sailed with her husband.

"Hello Mrs Blackburn," said the guard. "I have settled down now, too old for the sea. But what brings you to this fearsome place?"

"I have a message for a prisoner from his wife and children in the colonies. His name is Bill Lane. He is a friend of my nephew who was released from this prison some months ago." Mrs. Blackburn replied.

"Your nephew was in this prison?".

"Yes," replied Mrs Blackburn. "His name is Peter Walsh. He is the son of my late husband's sister. She went to the colonies many years ago and Peter was born in America. Peter was imprisoned because of this silly war between us and the colonies. I don't understand why Englishmen should be at war with other Englishmen!"

Tom wanted to avoid a political discussion with Mrs. Blackburn. "I suppose the King and parliament know what's best for us," he said. "Come with me Mrs. Blackburn and I will ask the duty officer to let you meet the prisoner."

Tom led her to the front office and told the duty officer of Mrs. Blackburn's request.

"Is she a relative of the prisoner?" asked the duty officer. "Only close relatives are allowed to see the prisoners."

"She is not a relative, Sir. But she is the widow of a sea captain who was well respected in these parts."

"You know the rules, Tom," said the duty officer. "But since she is a friend of yours I'll make an exception in her case."

"Come with me Mrs Blackburn. I'll take you to the prisoner."

Pixel followed them down a hallway to a corridor which had prison cells on either side. Near the top of each cell door was a small opening through which guards could communicate with the prisoners. The duty officer stopped at one door and called through the opening "Visitor for Bill Lane! Visitor for Bill Lane!"

When Bill appeared at the opening Mrs. Blackburn gave him the message from Mary. She told him about her nephew, Peter. She promised that she would write to Mary and tell her that Bill was in good health. And, when she saw that Bill was crying, she promised that she would make a return visit. Then she left quickly, she did not want Bill to see her cry.

Pixel now knew the location of Bill's cell. He had to fly to Bill's cell through its iron barred window in the rear wall of the prison to get his first look at him. Bill was sitting in a corner of the cell reading Mary's letter. His shoulders were hunched in despair.

Pixel rested on the roof of the prison while he considered his next step. And that's when he noticed that there were prisoners in an open yard behind the cells. Some of the prisoners were washing their clothes in a stone cistern beside a water pump in the prison yard. A few were playing a game with a ball that seemed to be made of straw and old clothes. As he watched, a bell sounded, and the prisoners in the yard started returning to their cells. A few minutes later more prisoners were led out to the prison yard, and an hour later they were returned to their cells. At sundown, when the last batch of prisoners returned to their cells, Pixel assumed that Bill must have exercised with prisoners earlier in the day.

That night, when Pixel was sure that all the prisoners in the cell were asleep, he flew to Bill's straw bed. Hovering behind Bill's ear, he started tickling Bill's nose with a piece of straw. It was very dark in the cell. When

Bill started stirring in his sleep Pixel whispered, "My name is Pixel. Pixel is Mary's friend. Watch for Pixel tomorrow at the water pump."

"Who's there?" said Bill when he was fully awake. "Who are you?"

Pixel whispered, "My name is Pixel. Pixel is Mary's friend. Watch for Pixel at the water pump. Good night, Bill."

"Where are you?" asked Bill. But there was no answer. Pixel had flown back to the spacecraft.

The British Naval officers who ran the prison wanted the prisoners to look after themselves as much as possible. It was easy to have them do their own washing in the prison yard. The prisoners had also built a clothes line along the wall close to the water pump. That is where Bill waited for the appearance of Pixel. After a sleepless night Bill had convinced himself that the voice in the dark was just a dream. Until he saw Sally's note. It fluttered to the prison floor when Bill picked up Mary's note in the morning. A tiny scrap of paper was tied neatly to a feather. The note, which had been delivered by Pixel, read: "LOVE SALLY."

Suddenly there was a commotion in the prison yard near the wall on the other side of the yard from the clothes line. Prisoners were shouting, "Up there! Look! What is it?"

What Bill saw was a melon like object flying back and forth above the heads of the prisoners! He was about to run across the yard to join the other prisoners when he heard a voice from the clothes line. "Bill stay here! I am Pixel ! Mary sent me to help you! Look behind you!"

When Bill turned around he was astonished to see a tiny greenish man hovering in front of the clothes line! "Pixel?" he asked, incredulously.

'Yes, Pixel. My name is Pixel. Mary sent me. Meet me here tomorrow. I will tell you more then."

Bill saw Pixel fly over the prison wall, and at the same time the melon like object roared into the sky and out of sight of the bewildered prisoners.

Bill was more than astonished. Mary's friend could fly! He was tiny! How did Mary meet him? This was not a dream, the other prisoners were talking excitedly about the object in the sky.

The prison bell sounded and the guards were trying to get the prisoners to return to their cells. But the prisoners just wanted to tell them what they saw. "It's a secret weapon developed by the French." said one prisoner.

"You should set us free before we are attacked again!" said another.

One of the guards had also seen the object, and he told the other guards what he saw. They eventually got the excited prisoners back to their cells.

When Bill and Pixel met at the clothes line the next morning Pixel did all the talking. He had prepared a speech. He said "Bill I will do all the talking today. I want to fly back to Mary with a message from you. My flying carriage will take me to Mary in less than six hours. Wait for me here every morning. I will answer all your questions. Trust me. What is your message for Mary?"

Bill was startled, but he quickly said, "Tell Mary I love her. Tell Adam and Sally I love them too."

And Pixel was gone.

THE PLAN

The family celebration lasted all evening. There were tears and laughter when Pixel showed the family the videos of the prison on the Isle of Wight. They wanted details of everything that happened. The family praised Mrs. Blackburn, laughed at the prisoners who were awed by the flying carriage, and cried when they saw their father, disconsolate in his cell. They were overjoyed when they saw Pixel's final video of Bill, sending his message of love.

The following morning Mary told Pixel what she had learned in the village.

"Both the blacksmith and the shopkeeper think I should delay going to Boston until the war is over. The blacksmith is confident that we will soon win the war; prisoners will be exchanged at that time. The shopkeeper thinks it would be unwise to sell the farm."

"What do you plan to do Mary?" asked Pixel. "What should I tell Bill on my next visit?"

"I really don't know what to do," said Mary. "I have no money for the trip to Boston. I would have to sell the farm. I would have to get a job in Boston while I tried to get Bill free. It could take months. I am not sure that Bill would want me to sell the farm."

"Is that what you want me to tell Bill?"

"No Pixel," Mary replied. "I have a better idea. I will write a letter to Bill explaining my dilemma. From what you told us last night you should be able to deliver the letter directly to Bill in his cell. Is that possible Pixel?"

"Yes," said Pixel. "That's a wonderful idea, Mary. Sally and I can work out the best way of tying the message."

"Pixel, this would be a great help to me," said Mary. "If Bill wants me to go to Boston, that's what I'll do. I will sell the farm immediately."

"I will take the letter to Bill." Pixel assured Mary. "But I have an idea too. It's a very dangerous idea. There may be another way to get Bill free."

Mary was startled. "Get Bill free? What do you mean Pixel?"

'It's just an idea Mary. I thought about it on my flight from the Isle of Wight. Before I tell you more I would like Adam to help me with an experiment. Can you delay sending your letter for a few days?"

"Is this another carriage contraption?" Mary asked, teasingly. She had become very confident in Pixel and his clever devices. "Of course we can wait. I trust you, Pixel."

For the rest of the morning Adam and Pixel worked near the woodpile creating the new contraption. They tested it at the river in the afternoon.

Adam had cut down a small tree for Pixel's experiment. It was about twenty feet tall with thick, bushy branches. It was lying on the river bank when Mary and Sally arrived the next morning for Pixel's demonstration.

They watched Adam as he tied a rope to the tree and attached the other end of the rope to the spacecraft's retractable cable.

"You've seen this before," Pixel explained. "This is exactly how Adam and I have collected trees all summer. Mary, I just want you to see the power of the flying carriage."

Pixel got into the spacecraft and started lifting the tree from the river bank. The tree swayed awkwardly at the end of the cable as Pixel carried it to the middle of river. There he slowly lowered it into the water. The tree drifted swiftly in the fast current. It seemed to Mary and Sally that Pixel had lost control, and that the tree was dragging the flying carriage downstream.

Mary was terrified. "Be careful, Pixel," she gasped.

Sally ran down the river bank shouting "Come back, Pixel! Come back!"

Adam ran after Sally. "Don't worry Sally," he shouted. "Pixel is safe. We did this yesterday. Pixel will return. Just watch."

They watched the spacecraft being dragged downstream until it disappeared from view at a bend in the river. Sally and Mary were terrified.

"Pixel will be back," said Adam, reassuringly. "We did this yesterday, just wait and see."

Just then the spacecraft reappeared. It was pulling the tree up the river, against the current. Pixel lifted the tree from the river and landed it beside Mary on the river bank. Adam quickly removed the rope from the spacecraft's cable.

"What do you think, Mary?" Pixel asked, as he emerged from the flying carriage.

"Please don't frighten me like that again." said Mary, reprovingly. "Pixel, I know you mean well but I was very worried for you."

"I'm sorry. Mary. I did not mean to frighten you. I just wanted to demonstrate the power of the flying carriage."

"I know you meant well," Mary assured Pixel. "But still I was very frightened."

"The second part of the demonstration will be even more frightening. But very safe. Adam and I tested it many times yesterday. Adam I think you should explain the next step."

"I'm sorry we frightened you, Mom." Adam was attaching another rope to the retractable cable. "It was my idea to let the tree drift down the river. I just wanted to impress you and Sally."

Pixel used the remote control to raise the spacecraft so that Adam's new rope contraption was swinging freely. It was about seven feet high. The seat of the swing, formed by two knots in the rope, hung about six inches above ground. It reminded Mary of the swing her father had made for her; she swung on it under an old oak tree in the backyard of the farm.

"Watch this, Mom," said Adam, proudly, as he stepped onto the seat of the swing while holding on to the rope with both hands. Mary and Sally watched in awe as the spacecraft carried Adam up and down the river bank.

"It's quite safe, Mom," Adam said confidently as he stepped off the swing. "Why don't you try it?"

Mary felt quite at ease with the swing. "Why not?" she said. "But not too high Pixel, I'm afraid of heights."

Sally thought her mother looked quite graceful in her long dress as she glided through the air. "Can I try too?" she asked.

Sally giggled as she flew in wider and wider circles around Mary and Adam. "I'm getting dizzy!" she yelled at Pixel.

When Sally landed it was time for the final demonstration. Adam stepped on the swing. "This part may look dangerous, Mom," he said, "but it is really quite safe. Pixel and I practiced this many times yesterday. Are you ready Mom?"

"If you are confident son, I will be brave."

"Let's do it," Adam nodded to Pixel.

The spacecraft lifted Adam about twenty feet in the air and carried him slowly across the river. Adam stepped off the rope swing on the far side of the river and waved in triumph to Sally and Mary.

"Congratulations, Pixel," said Mary, nervously. "I understand the power of the flying carriage. Now please bring Adam back to this side of the river."

There was no mention of an escape plan in Mary's letter to Bill. She was concerned that the letter might be seized by a guard. It was agreed that Pixel would discuss escape plans with Bill.

"I will return here as soon as Bill makes a decision." Pixel assured Mary, as he prepared to leave for the Isle of Wight.

"Just make sure that Bill understands that I am willing to sell the farm and go to Boston." Mary reminded Pixel. "The flying carriage is powerful, Pixel, but remember I have grave concerns about your rescue plan."

"I understand, Mary." said Pixel.

It was after midnight when Pixel landed the spacecraft in the prison yard, just beneath Bill's cell window. He flew to the cell window, carrying Mary's message around his neck in the thread halter that Sally had made. He placed the message on Bill's straw filled pillow.

"I have a message from Mary," Pixel whispered. Bill awoke in a daze. "What! Who?" he exclaimed.

"I am Mary's friend. I am Pixel. I will be in the prison yard tomorrow. I will answer all your questions."

Bill looked around the cell. It was too dark to see Pixel. "Where are you? Pixel?" asked Bill, desperately.

"Tomorrow, Bill. In the prison yard. Find a quiet place. I will land on your shoulder." Pixel whispered. "I will answer all your questions."

In the prison yard next morning Bill was pestered by the prisoner who slept beside him in the prison cell. "I heard you speaking out in your sleep last night. It sounded like you were softly singing. What were you dreaming?"

"I can't remember," said Bill. "But I didn't sleep well. I need to find a quiet corner to rest."

When Bill finally found a place away from other prisoners he sat on the ground and pretended to be reading his messages. Pixel landed on his shoulder.

"Don't say a word," Pixel whispered. "I will tell everything that you need to know. I flew to Earth from another planet in the flying carriage that you saw last week in the prison yard. I will tell you how I met Mary when we have more time. Mary has not yet found a way to get you released. She has explained all that in the letter I left with you last night. I think I may be able to help you escape from this prison by using some of the special powers in my flying carriage. But it would be very dangerous. It might not work. Mary wants you to know that she is very concerned about the rescue plan. She wants you to decide. I am going to stay on the Isle of Wight for a few days. I will come here every morning. Tomorrow I will answer any questions you may have. If you decide against the rescue plan

I will still bring you messages from Mary. So you do not have to decide right away."

Bill whispered, "I want to leave this place. I would like to hear your plan."

"I will tell you more tomorrow," said Pixel.

Pixel spent part of the day exploring the Isle of Wight and the south coast of England. He flew across the English Channel to explore the French ports. By the end of the day he had a plan that he thought might work. He discussed his plan with Bill in daily meetings in the prison yard. Bill offered suggestions. They both decided that the plan could work and Bill agreed that Pixel should go back to America and discuss it with Mary.

While Pixel was on the Isle of Wight, Mary made another visit to the village. She wanted to learn more about the war. She met a young couple from Boston who were heading west to set up a new farm on the frontier. The wife's father was one of the patriots who had fought under the leadership of George Washington in Boston; she was proud of her father and the other militiamen who had forced the British to withdraw from Boston. When Mary thought of the young men who were fighting and dying for a noble ideal she realized that her problems, in comparison, were trivial. She supported the escape plan that Bill had approved. It would be her family's small contribution to the war against the British.

ESCAPE

The flight to the Isle of Wight took much longer than usual. Adam had tied the rope swing securely to the spacecraft, but Pixel was concerned that, at high speed, wind vibration might loosen the knots. It took several days for the spacecraft to cross the Atlantic; Bill waited anxiously.

Around midnight Pixel landed the spacecraft, with the rope swing attached, in the prison yard. He flew immediately to Bill's cell. "Ready, Bill?" whispered Pixel, hovering close to Bill's ear.

Bill had been dozing fitfully. "Ready," he murmured, instantly alert.

Pixel began slicing through one of the iron bars in the cell window with the solar powered laser tool. The laser beam was powerful and soundless. In a few minutes the top of the iron bar was severed. Pixel made sure that there was a wide gap between the top of the severed bar and the brick wall. He did the same for the other two iron bars. The bottoms of the iron bars were only partially severed; Pixel did not want them to fall into the cell.

He used the remote device to raise the spacecraft slowly so that it was hovering in front of the cell window, with the rope swing floating freely from the retractable cable. He positioned the spacecraft so that the bottom of the rope swing was hanging just a bit lower than the tops of the iron bars. It was time for the most difficult manoeuvre. He had practised this step in his plan over and over at the cabin, with Adam congratulating him when he succeeded and encouraging him when he failed. Tonight he had to succeed.

Pixel flew to the bottom of the rope swing and used his shoulders to push it towards the severed iron bar. It was a very awkward move, Pixel was pushing on the rope and at the same controlling the hovering spacecraft with his remote device. The rope swing shifted as the hovering spacecraft reacted to changes in the wind. Finally Pixel was able to loop the rope swing over the first severed iron bar. The spacecraft was then lowered so that the bottom of the rope swing was pulling the iron bar towards the prison yard. Pixel used the power of the spacecraft to bend the iron bar slightly, so that it was leaning towards the ground in the prison yard. He repeated this procedure for each iron bar. Pixel then used the laser gun to completely sever each iron bar. They fell with resounding thuds into the prison yard; the cell window was now wide open for Bill.

Bill's neighbour awoke with a start. "What's that?" he exclaimed. "Bill, did you hear that?"

"You're dreaming, Rob" said Bill angrily. "Go back to sleep."

Pixel positioned the spacecraft so that the bottom of the rope swing was floating in front of the cell window. He used his shoulder to push the end rung of the rope swing through the cell window. As the spacecraft was lowered the swing drifted down the cell wall. Bill could see the swing, but Rob was still awake, muttering.

"I am trying to get some sleep, Rob. You had a nightmare." said Bill, hoping that Rob would not notice the swing.

Pixel had anticipated this problem. Mission Control had provided him with a stun gun to protect him from wild animals. Would it work with giants? He hovered to Rob and fired a tiny dart that penetrated deep into his neck.

"Damn!' said Rob, grasping at his neck.

"What's the matter?" asked Bill.

"Something's bitten me. It's very sore," he said, rubbing his neck vigorously. "I feel very sleepy."

Bill crawled over to Rob's bed of straw. "Are you alright, Rob?" he whispered. There was no answer.

Bill reached up and grasped the bottom rung of the swing and Pixel raised the spacecraft slowly so that Bill was pulled up the side of the cell wall. He crawled through the window and jumped to the prison yard. The spacecraft hovered above him. He grabbed hold of the rope swing and the spacecraft carried him across the prison yard, over the wall, and down to the wharf.

Bill was free!

Pixel landed the spacecraft on the wharf and opened the rear door so that Bill could get a small knife that had been stored inside by Adam.

There were three small boats moored at the wharf. They were the boats used by prison guards to transport prisoners to and from the British Navy warships moored at the large wharf further down the beach. This small wharf was for prison use only. Bill chose the smallest of the three boats. He loosened the boat's rope from its mooring on the wharf and passed it through the large iron ring that Adam had attached to the retractable cable. He tied the rope securely to the bow of the boat. The spacecraft could now pull the boat, just like the tree in Pixel's experiment on the river.

The final step was Bill's idea. He cut a length of rope from the mooring line of another boat, wound one end of the rope around his waist, and tied the other end to the rope swing. If he fell out of the boat he would still be in contact with the spacecraft. At worst he would get wet as the spacecraft pulled him through the sea.

They were now ready for the voyage to France.

The spacecraft flew about six feet above the sea. It pulled the small boat by the bowline which Bill had attached to the retractable cable. The rope swing, that was attached to the retractable cable and to the rope that Bill had wrapped around his waist, was flapping in the wind. If someone had seen this bizarre image from the shore they would have questioned their sanity. But it was three o'clock in the morning and the good people of the Isle of Wight were all sensibly in bed.

The sea was relatively calm as Pixel towed the boat out of the harbour. He kept the spacecraft at a slow and steady speed, going too fast made the boat very unstable and likely to capsize. At the speed they were travelling Pixel estimated that they would reach the port of Le Havre by mid-day.

But Bill was having a problem in the boat. The flapping of the rope swing was causing him to be constantly adjusting his balance in the boat, as the rope tugged at his waist. He realized now that he had made a mistake in tying himself to the rope swing. It was a good safety measure but it made the boat unstable. There was no way that Bill could discuss the problem with Pixel. Pixel could not leave the spacecraft, he had to be constantly steering to adapt to the wind and the shifting wave levels. Bill decided that untying the rope that attached him to the rope swing would solve the problem. He reasoned that if the boat capsized he could grab hold of the rope swing while Pixel tried to right the boat. In the worst case Pixel could drag the overturned boat and the rope swing, with Bill holding on, to shore. Bill was a very good swimmer and was very confident of Pixel's skills. So Bill loosened the rope around his waist, and the rope swing fluttered freely in the wind.

Pixel was alarmed when the onboard television camera showed Bill untying himself from the rope swing. But he respected Bill's judgement.

Bill enjoyed his new freedom. Pixel was pulling the boat smoothly across the relatively calm waters of the English Channel. Bill was so relaxed that he laid down on his back in the boat, and with the rope as a pillow, was soon fast asleep.

It was almost sunrise when Bill awoke from his nap. The sea was a little more choppy now, but Pixel was very adept in handling the waves. Bill was exhilarated. The clean sea breeze, the glorious sunrise, thoughts of Mary and his children, Pixel, and the amazing escape. Bill was truly in a joyous mood.

By mid-morning Pixel could see the coast of France on the horizon. But the waves were getting higher, and the boat was in danger of being swamped. Bill could see the danger. He was trying to get hold of the rope swing, but it was waving crazily in the wind, and out of his reach. Bill realized that it would be best to lie flat in the boat so that he could not easily be thrown overboard. This would be one less worry for Pixel as he tried to steer through the gusty winds.

Suddenly the winds grew stronger. Pixel tried to react, but a huge wave washed over the boat and turned it upside down in the water. Pixel was terrified. In the video monitor he could see the capsized boat, but there was no sign of Bill. Perhaps Bill was entangled in the rope! Pixel could use the spacecraft to lift the boat completely out of the water but he did not want to do this until he was sure that Bill was clear of the boat. What would he tell Mary? What should he do? Pixel circled the upturned boat; desperately hoping that Bill would surface.

And then a picture of Bill appeared on the video monitor. He was quite a distance from the boat and was floating on the two oars that had been stowed in the bottom of the boat. When the boat capsized Bill immediately realized that he might need the oars. So he stayed under the boat and struggled to get the oars free. He had to surface for air several times before he was able to free the oars.

Pixel flew the spacecraft towards Bill and lowered the spacecraft close enough to the waves so that the bottom of the rope swing was touching the sea. In the turbulent water it was impossible for Bill to get hold of the swing. He was getting very cold. The boat was still upended and bouncing in the water close to the swing. Pixel tried to keep the spacecraft directly above Bill, but the wind and waves meant that he had to be constantly adjusting his position. Sometimes Bill drifted far away from the swing and the boat. Finally Pixel moved the spacecraft so that the boat bumped into Bill. He seized the bow rope and was able to lie astraddle the overturned boat. He was cold and exhausted, but he was safe.

Pixel knew that they were very close to France. But dragging the overturned boat was going to be difficult and slow. Bill was in a very awkward position, he was having a difficult time hanging on to the bowline. Pixel thought he could right the boat by pulling it completely out of the water and then setting it down again. But would Bill understand what he was trying to do? Could Bill hold on? Pixel decided to try. As the boat was raised slowly out of the water the swing came within Bill's reach.

Bill pulled himself on to the swing. As Pixel lowered the boat back into the sea Bill used his feet to make the boat float right side up in the water. He lowered himself into the boat and held onto the swing while Pixel headed for shore.

They landed on a sandy beach, quite a few miles away from Le Havre. The winds had weakened, but it was raining steadily and Bill was very cold.

"I saw a farm house just before we had our little accident," said Pixel. "If you untie the swing from the flying carriage I will find the closest farm house."

"Hurry Pixel," said Bill, as he loosened the ropes. "I'm freezing cold!"

Pixel flew over a low, steep cliff behind the beach and immediately saw the farm house. It was at the far side of a wheat field that ended at the edge of the cliff. Pixel returned to Bill, gave him directions, and said, "I will fly over to the farm house to see if anyone's there."

"I won't be long," said Bill, shivering as he hurried down the beach.

A barn with a hay loft was close to the house. The farmer was not in the barn so Pixel parked the spacecraft in the hay loft. The farm was occupied by an older couple who were both in the kitchen. The farmer was sitting close to a window and his wife was cooking.

Pixel flew back to Bill with the good news. "What shall I say to them?" asked Bill, running quickly to stay warm. "I only know two expressions in French: *Je suis anglais* and *parlez-vous anglais*."

"I'm sure they will help." said Pixel.

When the farmer's wife opened the door Bill blurted out, "I'm American. Help me. I'm American"

"An American." she cried, in French. "An American, Pierre. The man is freezing to death! Pierre get him some warm clothes."

She led Bill by the hand into the kitchen and immediately gave him some warm broth that she had on the stove. Pierre ran upstairs for a blanket, an old shirt and faded coveralls. The wife insisted that Bill change into her husband's clothes, in the kitchen, by the wood fire. She looked out the kitchen window so that Bill would not be embarrassed. The couple talked excitedly to each other and to Bill who, of course understood almost nothing of what they said. He did learn that their names were Pierre and Marie, and they understood that his name was Bill and that he was going to Le Havre, but did not know how to get there.

Bill had a wonderful evening with Pierre and Marie. Marie served him a mouth watering supper, and he and Pierre finished a bottle of home-made wine. He slept that night on the floor of their small living room. It was a memorable first night of freedom. Pixel slept in the barn, with the horses and cows, and wondered what they should do in Le Havre.

The next day, after breakfast, Marie prepared a parcel for Bill that included a loaf of bread, some cheese, and a jug of water.

"For our brave American friend." she exclaimed, in French. She and Pierre said goodbye to Bill and pointed him on the road to Le Havre.

LE HAVRE

━━◦▰◦━━

Bill was whistling as he walked down the dirt road to Le Havre.

Freedom. It was an intoxicating feeling to be walking in the clean, cool air,

with an open sky, and no walls. On one side of the road was a wheat field,

on the other a forest whose trees were beginning to shed their leaves.

His whistling ended when the spacecraft flew into view and landed in the

forest, a few feet from the road. When Pixel hovered to Bill he said, "Good

morning, Bill. I think you had a very pleasant evening?"

"Pixel! Pixel!" Bill exclaimed. "How can I ever thank you? I had a

wonderful evening. You are an extraordinary person. You are incredibly

brave. Thank you. Thank you. I will do anything I can to repay the debt I

owe you."

Pixel was proud, but very humble. "Bill, I am glad to help. The people

on my planet love helping others. Adam saved my life. Your family has

taught me how to speak your language. Mary has been very patient and

kind. I will be very happy to see you safely home."

"Adam saved your life? Tell me about it, Pixel. I have so many

questions."

"There is much to tell you, Bill. But I am anxious about what we will do

in Le Havre. I think we should have a plan."

100

"I am sure that there will be an American ship in the harbour," said Bill. "They always need experienced sailors. I might even get a position as first mate. I hope they will give me an advance to buy new shoes and clothes."

"Are you not afraid that a British warship may seize this ship and return you to the prison?"

"Yes there is that danger." Bill replied. "But from what I have heard in prison the war with France is keeping the British Navy very busy protecting their own trading ships. It's a chance that I will have to take. There is no other way for me to get home."

"I have something to show you," said Pixel. "I flew to Le Havre early this morning and made images of the boats in the harbour. Perhaps you can tell if any of the ships are American."

"Images? What do you mean? Images?" asked Bill.

"Moving images is what Mary calls them. They are like paintings. They are inside the flying carriage; I think you will be able to see them. Just a moment Bill and I will show you what to do."

Pixel flew to the spacecraft which was parked on a bed of leaves. He opened the rear door, lowered the exit ramp, and ran inside. Bill knelt on the forest floor to get a better view of Pixel's images. He was very surprised to see Pixel driving the all-terrain vehicle down the ramp.

"What is that contraption?" asked Bill. "Is that what you a call an image? It looks like a horseless carriage."

"No that's not an image. I'm not sure what to call it. But Adam and Sally think it's a wonderful toy. It was designed to help me explore your planet. But I find flying to be much better."

"And the images? Where are they?" Bill was quite puzzled The only images that he knew were religious paintings that he had seen in churches.

"Bill, the images are inside the flying carriage. All you have to do is pick up the flying carriage, with both hands, and look inside. Tell me what you see."

The video monitor in the spacecraft was about the size of a postage stamp. It normally showed real time images from cameras built into all sides of the spacecraft. Pixel had programmed the monitor to display a half hour video he had made, that morning, of the sailing ships in the port of Le Havre.

"You want me to pick up the flying carriage?" asked Bill, timidly.

"Yes. I'm sure it's not too heavy. But it would be best not to touch the exit ramp. Just pick it up and look inside."

Bill picked up the spacecraft very carefully. The sides were smooth and firm. The front of the spacecraft was shaped like the leading edge of a bullet. The rear, where the exit ramp hung loose, was straight. Bill could look directly into the spacecraft through the opening at the exit ramp.

"I can see ships in a harbour! I can see ships at a dock. Many ships have the French flag—the fleurs-de-lis. Am I looking at Le Havre?"

"Yes," said Pixel. "Those are images I made from a device built into the flying carriage."

Bill was astonished. "They look so real. And they do move. Moving images! I can see the flags moving with the wind."

"Can you see any American ships? Can you see their flag?"

"I am not sure if there is an American flag. America is a new country. They may not have a flag. America is at war with Great Britain. If America loses the war they may no longer have a country." said Bill, sadly.

Bill placed the spacecraft gently on the forest floor. "Pixel, there is much magic in your flying carriage. Some of the ships might be American. I will just have to go to Le Havre and talk to the sailors. Is it far from here?"

Pixel thought of that first walk with Mary and the children. The distance to Le Havre was a bit less than the distance to the cabin from the Indian camp. "If you walked you could get there late this afternoon. But perhaps you could fly?"

"Fly? Pixel, do you mean with the rope swing?"

"Why not? There are only a few farms on our way to Le Havre. You would be flying over the forest most of the time. I would stop frequently so that you would not be too tired holding on."

"Pixel, I think it's a great idea. I could hold on with one hand and wave to you if I need a rest. But the rope swing is still at the beach. Do you want us to go back there?"

"No, Bill. I think I could use the flying machine to bring the rope swing here. If you could tie the string from one of your shoes to the cable on the flying carriage I could attach the rope swing to the string and fly it back here. You could then attach the rope swing more securely to the iron ring on the cable. I should tell you that Adam designed that iron ring. Your son is very clever."

"Pixel, you are brilliant. You think of everything. Let's do it. I can show you a sailor's knot that is very easy to make."

When Pixel had retrieved the rope swing, and Bill had secured it to the iron ring, it was time to fly. Bill was confident that there would be no need to stop during the flight to Le Havre. But he agreed that, if he got tired, he would wave to Pixel. Bill had made an important change to the rope swing. He had shaped a broken branch with his knife to create a seat. When the shaped branch was wedged between the two strands of the rope it resulted in a seat not unlike the seat in a park swing. It was too rough to sit on, but when Bill stood on the "seat" he looked somewhat like a circus performer in a trapeze.

When he had Bill airborne Pixel flew quite slowly over the trees. He wanted to be sure that Bill was safe. But the onboard video monitor showed that Bill was having fun. So Pixel increased the speed of the spacecraft. When they flew over their first farm there was no one in the field. But in the next field a farmer was coming out of his barn just as Bill flew by.

"*Bonjour monsieur!*" shouted Bill to the farmer.

"*Bonjour.*" said the startled farmer. He ran into the kitchen to tell his wife that he had seen a 'silver pumpkin flying with a man on a swing.'

"Jean, you must stop drinking so much wine," his wife replied, teasingly. "Flying pumpkin indeed!"

The flight to Le Havre took less than one hour. Pixel set Bill down in a forest just outside of the town.

"That was fun," said Bill happily. "I could see Le Havre while I was flying. It is just ahead of us, on the other side of a cliff."

"I know," said Pixel. "This is a good place for us to rest. I need to learn about sailing ships."

"This would be a good time to have some of the bread and cheese that Marie gave me. Pixel you should try this cheese. They say that the French make the best cheese in the world."

"I have never tried cheese. On my planet we only eat plants. What is cheese made from?"

"From cow's milk," said Bill. "When I get home I will buy Mary a cow so that we can make cheese for the family. Try it Pixel. You might like it."

To Pixel's surprise he did like cheese. And he enjoyed his lunch with Bill.

"Pixel, now that I am so close to Le Havre I think you should fly back to Mary with the good news of my escape. From what you have told me you can be there and back in less than one day. The voyage home across the Atlantic may take two to three months. Mary and the children will be happy to know that I am free and on my way home."

"I completely agree, Bill. As soon as you are safely on an American ship I will fly to Mary. But I have some ideas which might help you to avoid British warships. I'll explain the basic plan and then we can work out the details. We have to do this before you embark on your voyage. I may not be able to meet with you once you board the ship."

"I have been thinking about that," said Bill. "There may be a way for us to meet. If I get the position of first mate I might be able to get the night watch, and we could meet after midnight. But first I would like to hear your plan."

"Bill, it is a bit complicated. When you sail out to sea I can fly high above your ship to get a view of all the ships that are close to yours. The higher I fly the more ships I will be able to see. I can make an image of those ships, like the images you saw in the flying carriage, a sort of map of where each ship is positioned on the sea. The flying carriage has a device that can make those images, make that map. The flying carriage also has a device that can calculate the distance between your ship and every other ship that is in the overview picture. Once I have that image I can then fly close to each ship to determine whether or not it is a British battleship.

And I could report to you how far away the battleship is, and the direction it is sailing. Bill, does this make sense to you?"

"Pixel, I can't imagine a device that can make images and calculate distances. But if you can tell me when a British battleship is close, and the direction it is sailing, that would be a great help."

"That's where I need your help, Bill. How can I identify a British battleship compared to a French battleship? What is the difference between a battleship and a trading ship? How can I tell one from the other?"

"The big difference between a battleship and a trading ship is cannons. Battleships have cannons, seventy cannons and more on some British battleships. Trading ships have no cannons."

"Cannons? I don't remember Mary using that word. What is a cannon?"

"I am not surprised that Mary did not teach you about cannons. Mary does not approve of guns, or wars. Cannons are used by battleships to sink or disable enemy battleships. Cannons are large guns that fire projectiles. They are deadly weapons."

"Bill, I have many questions about wars. There have never been wars on my planet. When you get home to America I hope you will tell me more about wars. But I still don't understand what a cannon looks like."

"I think it would be easier if I drew you a picture," said Bill as he cleared leaves from the ground and used a twig to sketch an outline of a sailing ship. "The cannon portholes are at the side of the ship, just below the deck. These ten holes represent ten cannons on this side of the ship. There would be ten guns on the other side of the ship. You would call this a twenty gun battleship. Pixel, you have an image of a battleship in your flying machine. I recognized a French battleship in the images you showed me."

"I think I know the ship you mean. I will review the pictures and you can tell me if I am right."

When Pixel viewed the images and identified the French battleship, he froze the battleship image on the video monitor. "Have another look, Bill. Is that a French battleship?"

Bill picked up the spacecraft. "Yes, Pixel. That's a battleship. A French battleship. A British battleship would be flying the Union Jack flag. This a picture of a Union Jack." Bill drew a rough outline of the British flag on the forest floor.

"Are there any other flags that I should worry about?" asked Pixel.

"I don't think so," said Bill. "The Spanish also have battleships, but Spain is not at war with America."

"Fine," said Pixel. "I will be able to recognize British battleships. But to get a message to you I will need to park the flying carriage somewhere on the ship. At night there might be a quiet deck where I could land the flying carriage, but it could easily slide into the sea as the ship rocked with the waves."

"I have an answer for you, Pixel. It just occurred to me when I saw the picture of the French battleship. Every sailing ship carries a number of small boats that are slung by ropes on booms off the main deck. The boats are used when the ships are in harbour to ferry goods and passengers to and from the dock. They are also used in emergencies. If the ship is sinking, for any reason, the boats could be used to rescue the sailors. You could land the flying machine in the bottom of any of these boats. Look again at the picture of the French battleship. I think you will see boats strung up alongside the main deck."

"Yes," said Pixel. "I can see the boats. When you walk down to Le Havre I will fly out to get a better look at the rescue boats on the battleship. There is one thing I do not understand about sailing ships. We have never had sailing ships on our planet. Our seas are really tiny compared to the seas on earth. I realize that the sails catch the power of the wind to move the ship forward. I do not understand how a ship can sail against the wind. Can you explain that to me?"

"I am not sure I can explain it, Pixel. I think it would be easier to show you when we meet on the ship. Can you wait?"

"Of course, Bill. We will have time in our midnight meetings. So if you are ready I think we should be on our way to Le Havre. I will fly down and be watching to see what ship you choose. I will try to meet you, around midnight."

"Pixel, you may be flying to Mary in a few days. Please tell her how much I love her. And tell her to kiss Adam and Sally for me."

Bill was crying quietly, and Pixel also wanted to cry. Instead he said, bravely, "I will, Bill."

"And Pixel, tell Mary that I really, really like the 'little friend' she sent to help me."

And with that, Pixel was crying too.

THE ATLANTIC

When Bill approached the four American sailors at the dock in Le Havre they at first thought he was a French beggar! He looked quite ragged with his overgrown beard, Pierre's old coat that was at least two sizes too small, and worn out trousers. But they were soon impressed by the amazing story that Bill told them of his escape from the prison in Great Britain. Of course Bill made no mention of Pixel in the story. If he had talked about Pixel's role they would have thought he was insane. Bill was a natural story teller and it was easy for him to create a plausible story of his single-handed escape.

The sailors were loading a small boat with supplies for their ship, named Freedom, moored in the harbour. They told Bill that the ship was bound for New York, stopping first in the French West Indies for a load of sugar. They were confident that their captain would take Bill back to America. They would row him out to meet their captain, Captain Bourne.

When the boat was close to the ship Bill was surprised to see that Freedom had four cannons. "I thought you said this was a trading ship," said Bill angrily. He thought that the sailors were trying to trick him to join a pirate's ship! "Why are there cannons on the ship? Is this a pirate ship?"

The sailors all laughed. One of them said, "Don't worry Bill, we are not pirates. This ship is a privateer. The new American government is encouraging us to defend ourselves against the British navy. The war has changed many things Bill. The captain will tell you more. Like you he was also captured by the British, and escaped. You can trust him."

Bill was still worried, but he sensed that the young sailors were honest Americans. He could dive overboard and swim back to shore or he could meet Captain Bourne. He decided to meet Captain Bourne.

When they boarded the Freedom they were met immediately by the captain. He was much older than Bill, with a stern expression, and a powerful voice. "Who is the wild man?" the captain asked.

"He is a brave American sailor, Captain Bourne. He has escaped from a British prison and rowed a boat, alone, across the English Channel, sir!" said one of the sailors. "His name is Bill."

"A likely story!" said the captain. 'Is it a true story, Bill?'

"Yes sir," said Bill. "I abandoned the boat on a beach just north from Le Havre. A kindly French farmer gave me these old clothes as mine were lost in a storm. The prison was on the Isle of Wight."

"I have heard of that prison." said Captain Bourne. "Bill, come into my cabin. I would like to hear your story."

When Bill told his story to Captain Bourne he emphasized his career at sea. He told him of his earnest desire to see his family again. He down-played his escape.

"I am impressed, Bill." said the captain. "One day I will tell you how I escaped from the British. I already have a first mate but I can use a man with your experience."

"Thank you, captain. I will help in any way I can."

"Before you accept Bill, I should tell you that this ship is a privateer. Do you know what that means?"

"No sir, I do not."

"It's this terrible war, Bill. The British Navy is trying to stop trade ships from bringing supplies to America. They use their battleships to seize or destroy American trading ships. The new American government does not have a navy, they have no ships to fight the British battleships. So the American government has given privately owned ships, like the Freedom, permission to seize British trading ships. The American government will give a reward to any privateer that captures a British ship."

"It sounds like piracy, sir."

"Yes it is Bill. Legalized piracy. But you should know that when we reach the West Indies I will be trying to seize a British trade ship. Every member of my crew is aware of my plan. Everyone will share in the reward. They all know there is danger."

"There is also danger if I sailed on a ship that was not a privateer." said Bill.

"That's true, Bill. But you have a family. It is your decision to make. I like you. I am going to loan you money to buy new clothes in Le Havre.

You look terrible in the farmer's old clothes. I will have someone row you back to the dock. If you decide to join us there will be boats from Freedom going back and forth to Le Havre all evening. We leave for the West Indies in the morning. If you decide not to join us I expect you to repay me. Some time, somewhere, after the war. Good luck, Bill!"

"Thank you, captain. You are very kind."

During all his years at sea Bill had never met any pirates. But he had heard stories in which sailors had been tricked into becoming pirates. That was his first thought when he saw the cannons. What Captain Bourne said about privateers made sense to Bill. And the captain was honest and open about the risks of being a privateer. Bill wanted to say yes to the captain's offer, but he felt he should discuss it first with Pixel. He was sure Pixel would meet him when he went ashore. So after buying clothes from a haberdasher that specialized in ship supplies Bill strolled through the town and sat down on a park bench.

"Hello, Bill! You look wonderful in your new clothes."

Bill looked up to see Pixel sitting comfortably in the crook of a tree. "Pixel. I knew you would find me. I met the captain of an American ship that leaves tomorrow. But there is a problem."

"I know your concern, Bill. I was in the captain's cabin when he spoke to you. Before you decide what to do I should tell you that I surveyed the sea around Le Havre while you were walking to town. The closest British battleships are five days away, and they are sailing south, away from Le Havre."

"That's good news, Pixel. If you can give me information like that, every night, it will be a big help. I am going to accept Captain Bourne's offer. Other Americans are taking grave risks in this war. I should be prepared to take risks for my country."

"I think you are making the right decision. Since the ship is not leaving before tomorrow I am going to fly to Mary today. I will find you on the Freedom, either tomorrow night or the next night."

"Yes, you should give Mary the news. Thank you Pixel."

"I have one more idea, Bill. If for any reason I cannot meet with you one night, and a battleship is close, I will fly my ship the next morning, very fast, in front of the Freedom. It will be a sign that you should follow the direction of the flying carriage to avoid contact with the battleship."

"It will startle Captain Bourne and the crew. But that's a good idea, Pixel."

"Then, safe journey, Bill.'

"Safe journey!" said Bill, as he left for the dock and his meeting with Captain Bourne.

It was early evening when Pixel arrived at the cabin. The weather was colder than Le Havre and Mary had a warm fire in the kitchen. He landed on the chicken coop into a colourful bed of Holly leaves and berries! Sally thought this would be a nice way to welcome Pixel home. Since Christmas was only a few weeks away, Mary agreed. She was not sure she would be able to explain Christmas to Pixel. She imagined the endless questions he would ask. But the beautiful floral arrangement worked. Pixel had to compose himself, and wipe away tears, before he flew into the cabin.

"Pixel's home!' Sally shouted as he landed on the kitchen table. "Is our Dad safe? When is he coming home? Will he be here for Christmas? Pixel we are so happy to see you!"

"Your Dad is safe. He is on a ship called Freedom that is sailing to the West Indies and then to New York. I have a lot to tell you."

"Thank you Pixel." said Mary. "We have been so worried. Please tell us everything that happened. We'll try to be calm, won't we children?" Mary really wanted to hug Pixel. And so did Sally who, ever so gently tried to stroke Pixel's long hair. Pixel squirmed and Mary immediately said, "Sally I am sure Pixel knows how much we love him. I don't think he wants to be patted."

"I am very ticklish." said Pixel, feeling quite overwhelmed, but exceedingly happy with the loving attention.

"Pixel, I really want to know about the prison escape. Did it work exactly as planned?" asked Adam. "Do you have pictures to show us?"

"Yes I do have pictures, Adam. But let me tell you the whole story and then I will show you some pictures of your Dad."

"Let's give Pixel a chance to tell us his story." said Mary.

"I will begin with the prison escape." said Pixel who then gave them a detailed account of his adventures with Bill. Sally and Adam had endless questions. Mary listened seriously but burst into laughter when Pixel told them how Bill, while flying over the barn, had waved to the farmer. Pixel finished his story by explaining his plan for tracking British battleships.

"You will be able to warn Bill if there are any British battleships close to his ship?' Mary asked.

"That is the plan. Mary. That's why I am leaving early in the morning. I want to be sure that I can locate Freedom and start monitoring for battleships."

"I am ready for the pictures!" Adam declared.

"Yes, could we please see the pictures, Pixel?" asked Sally. "I do want to see Dad flying over the trees!"

"Adam please blow out the candle and I'll start the pictures now."

Pixel had carefully edited the pictures in the spacecraft's computer database to show highlights of the escape. The children were thrilled with the show. Mary was filled with wonder at the magic of the little man. When she saw Bill having a happy meal with Pierre and Marie she burst into tears of joy. And Adam and Sally hugged her with tears of their own.

It was well after midnight when Mary insisted that the children allow Pixel to get some sleep.

"I do want to make an early start tomorrow," said Pixel. "I am not sure how long it will take the Freedom to get to New York. But as soon as Bill is safely in America I will fly to you."

"Good night Pixel, and good luck!" said Mary, affectionately.

During his return flight to the Freedom Pixel wondered about Mary and her life in the cabin. It seemed to him that the French couple, Pierre and Marie, had a better, somehow richer life than Mary and her family. The French family had a barn with cows and two horses. The food they served seemed more interesting. They had a small parlour with books. They had a chimney for their fire, so the rooms were smoke free. Pixel wondered if there was anything that he could do to make life better for his family. But first he would have to get Bill safely home to America.

The first mate of the Freedom was very pleased to get an experienced sailor like Bill as his assistant. He was even more pleased when Bill volunteered for the midnight watch. And so Bill was on the quarterdeck on his first night at sea. The ship had stayed close to the French shore until it reached the port of Brest. From there it left the English Channel and sailed into the boundless waters of the Atlantic ocean.

"Hello, Bill," said Pixel softly. He was sitting on a sail just above Bill's head. "You seem to be deep in thought."

"You are right Pixel. I was thinking of the amazing adventure we have had over the last three days. I was thinking how lucky I am to be sailing home."

"Mary and Sally and Adam send their love. The children loved the pictures of you flying. Mary thought it was very gracious of you to wave to the French farmer."

"Thanks, Pixel, it will be so good to see them again."

"I have good news about the battleships. They are now six days away and are heading in a westerly direction. I think the Freedom is on more southerly route?"

"Yes, we are heading to the West Indies. The British battleships are probably going to New York, or to Halifax."

"Bill I will give you a more detailed report tomorrow. I am very tired."

"I will meet you at the same place. Good night, Pixel."

Over the next two weeks Pixel had very little to report. He had seen a convoy of five British trade ships, escorted by a battleship, heading north to Britain. Bill thought they must be loaded with sugar from Jamaica. In their midnight meetings Bill did teach Pixel a lot about sailing. Pixel learned how a ship could sail against the wind by tacking, that is by zigzagging into the wind to reach the final destination. He learned the importance of the rudder. Bill took Pixel to the special room below the captain's cabin to see the ship's tiller. The tiller was a long sturdy oak pole that was attached to the ship's rudder by a strong metal clasp. It needed two sailors to move the tiller back and forth, as directed by the captain. The night that Pixel saw the tiller it was held in place by two ropes attached to oak beams.

"When the tiller is locked in place by ropes it means that the captain has determined that the ship should be on a steady course," Bill explained. "In the morning the captain might want to change course and the tiller would be manually adjusted until the captain is satisfied that the ship is moving in the right direction. That is how the boat is steered, Pixel. The wind is the power and the tiller, acting on the rudder, gives direction to the ship."

One night Pixel decided to explore a British battleship. He parked the spaceship in one of the rescue boats hoisted at the side of the ship and, on foot, made his way below the decks. He saw sailors sleeping in hammocks beside the cannons on the ship's gun deck. He explored the tiller room. He was very interested in exactly how the tiller was connected to the rudder. He spent some time in the captain's large cabin. It was dimly lit but Pixel could see maps and charts and a globe. He was surprised to see how incomplete the globe was compared to the images of earth that were stored on the spacecraft's computer.

Pixel now slept in the spacecraft while it was parked in one of Freedom's boats. He felt quite safe there; he found the gentle rocking of the boat quite soothing.

Early on the morning of their thirteenth day at sea, the rain started. The heavy raindrops activated the spacecraft's detection system and awoke Pixel who quickly flew the spacecraft out of the boat. As the winds increased Pixel had to fly high above the storm to retain control of the spacecraft. In his last report to Bill he had noted that a British sugar convoy, escorted by a British battleship, was two sailing days away, travelling north. With the storm raging below it was impossible for Pixel to track the convoy. The storm increased in intensity during the day and blew steadily during the night.

The storm diminished early the next morning and Pixel was able to take the spaceship down to the Freedom. He was surprised to see that the British battleship was quite close to the Freedom. In fact Bill and Captain Bourne had already sighted the battleship; it was trying to intercept the Freedom!

Captain Bourne was trying desperately to outmanoeuvre the battleship. But the battleship was gaining, steadily. Pixel's plan for warning Bill had been all in vain! His first thought was to fly the spacecraft, at great speed, back and forth in front of the battleship; but he doubted that such a manoeuvre would deter the British captain. He had to find a way to delay the battleship.

To avoid detection Pixel flew the spacecraft just above the waves to a rescue boat stowed at the stern of the battleship. In hover mode he landed the spacecraft in the rescue boat. He then flew to a mast overlooking the quarterdeck where the British captain was directing his officers and crew in hot pursuit of the Freedom. It seemed that no one had noticed the landing of the spacecraft. Just below the quarterdeck the helmsman was managing the tiller; he had four sailors moving the long wooden pole back and forth to keep the battleship on the course required by the captain.

Pixel flew into the opening, at the stern of the ship, where the rudder was connected to the tiller. A sturdy metal hinge connected the rudder to the tiller. Pixel hovered to the tiller, just beside the metal hinge. It was huge, several times taller than Pixel. It was impossible to stand on the tiller; Pixel could not maintain his balance as the long pole was shifted from side to side by the sailors, and up and down by the waves. Instead he crouched precariously on the tiller and, using his laser gun, started to bore holes in the hinge.

On the Freedom Captain Bourne was very worried. He could see that the battleship was gradually overtaking his ship. He was hoping that he could be still ahead by nightfall and escape in the darkness. Early in the afternoon the battleship fired a warning shot at the Freedom. The cannon ball landed quite far away from the Freedom.

"They are trying to frighten us," said Captain Bourne to Bill. "But we will give them a good fight!"

"I am sure we will escape," Bill replied, encouragingly. He was wondering about Pixel, what would he do?

The cannon shot startled Pixel. He was making some progress with the laser gun, but it was painfully slow. He kept slipping off the tiller. He tried using the laser gun in hover mode but it was impossible to aim accurately. He flew out to see if the Freedom had been hit. He was relieved to see that the battleship was still a long way from the Freedom. But the battleship was clearly gaining.

Pixel resumed his work with the laser gun. He was becoming quite frustrated with his efforts. He had bored several holes but not enough to weaken the hinge. He heard two more cannon shots. He continued boring, worried now that the solar battery in the laser gun might need to be recharged. Suddenly, the hinge snapped, the tiller was no longer connected to the rudder. The battleship stopped immediately. It rolled back and forth, aimlessly, in the waves. Pixel rushed to the spacecraft and blasted off triumphantly.

On the Freedom Bill was the first to notice that the battleship was no longer moving. "The battleship is in trouble, captain!"

"You are right Bill," said the captain when he viewed the battleship through his telescope. "She is taking down her sails. There must have been an accident, probably an explosion in the munitions room."

Bill was not so sure. He wondered where Pixel might be. Suddenly everyone on the Freedom was startled by an object that flew across the bow of the ship, at great speed!

"What was that?" exclaimed Captain Bourne.

Bill knew that it was Pixel, and he was signalling that they should be heading north west. Sailing in that direction would take them close to the disabled battleship. Was Pixel telling him that there was another battleship to the south of the Freedom?

"I can't tell," said Bill. "It happened so quickly."

"Whatever." said the captain. "We will head south and be thankful for His Majesty's misfortune."

"Could I make a suggestion, captain?" Bill asked.

"Of course." said Captain Bourne.

"When I first sighted the battleship I think that I also saw a trade ship just behind it. I am not sure but it is possible that the battleship was leading a convoy of sugar ships from Jamaica. If I am right then perhaps we should be heading north west. We might intercept an undefended sugar ship. It would save us the voyage to the West Indies."

"And get you home to your family sooner!" said the captain, with good humour. "But your idea has merit. We could spend weeks looking for a prize in the West Indies. It would not hurt to try. We'll head north-west. But Bill I want you to watch the battleship constantly. If there is any sign of movement let me know immediately."

Pixel was glad to see the Freedom change course. Four British trading ships were just over the horizon from the Freedom. They were presumably waiting for the return of the battleship to escort them safely to Britain. Pixel would give his report to Bill at midnight.

Bill was tired, but exceedingly happy, when the First Mate took over the duty watch the next morning. Pixel had confirmed, in their midnight meeting, that the battleship was still disabled and the unprotected sugar ships were only a few hours away. Captain Bourne would be pleased.

"They seem to be waiting for the battleship," said Captain Bourne to Bill and the first mate when the sugar ships were sighted. "Their sails are down."

Before giving chase to the Freedom the captain of the battleship had in fact signalled the trading ships, by flag, that they should wait for his return. Even when they sighted the Freedom the trading ships had delayed setting sail, they hoped that the battleship was still in pursuit. When they realized that the battleship was not coming to their rescue it was too late. The Freedom was soon close enough to one of the ships for Captain Bourne to order that a warning cannon shot be fired. The British ship immediately raised the white flag of surrender.

When the ships were quite close Captain Bourne ordered that one of the Freedom's small boats be lowered. "Why don't you come with me Bill?" asked the captain. "I think you will find this quite interesting."

"I would be glad to, captain." said Bill, as he scrambled down a rope ladder to join Captain Bourne in the row boat. Four sailors rowed them the short distance to the British ship.

"Request permission to come on board." Captain Bourne shouted when they reached the side of the British ship. He was enjoying the moment immensely.

The British captain, looking down on the row boat from the main deck replied, "Permission granted."

When Captain Bourne and Bill climbed to the main deck they were met by the British captain who said, angrily, "This is an outrage! We are an unarmed trading ship sailing in international waters. How dare you threaten us!"

"My name is Captain Bourne. I have been authorized by the government of the United States of America to seize enemy ships wherever they may be and deliver such ships to the American government. I am taking possession of this ship on behalf of the American government. What is your name captain?"

Before the British captain could reply a tall, well dressed gentleman appeared on the quarterdeck and said, "Captain Shaw, could I have a word with Captain Bourne? I can see that he is a man of determination."

"Captain Bourne, my name is Douglas Banks. I am called Sir Douglas Banks in England. I own a large sugar estate in Jamaica, and am part-owner of this ship and the other three ships in our little convoy. I am also a member of the British parliament. I was in parliament when the vote was taken as to whether or not we should go to war with our American colonies. You should know, Captain Bourne, that I and many other members voted against going to war. We thought it was a tragic mistake."

Captain Bourne was quite surprised by the speech. He had never met a British parliamentarian, and assumed that they all hated the American colonists. "It is a tragic war." he replied. "But it is a war. And I am bound to help my country win that war."

"Captain Bourne, I am not challenging your right to seize this ship. But I am concerned about the crew. And I am very concerned about my wife who is expecting the birth of a baby in four months. She is laying in her cabin right now very distressed as to what will happen to her."

"What are you proposing, Sir Douglas?" asked Captain Bourne respectfully. He had planned that the British crew would sail the ship to America, with Bill as captain. He was prepared to offer the British crew some of the prize money for their efforts. He had not planned for an expectant mother!

"My request, Captain Bourne is that you allow us to signal one of the other ships to sail back to meet us here. And I am requesting that you allow my wife and our crew be transferred to that ship. If you do that, sir, I will give you a promissory note for one thousand pounds."

"I am not sure that a note for a thousand British pounds will be worth anything now in America," said Captain Bourne, with a roar of laughter. But the plan made sense to him. He would not have to worry about the British crew and he was sure that Bill could manage the ship with a few crew members from the Freedom.

"But I accept your offer, Sir Douglas. With the provision that you and Captain Shaw be my guests on the Freedom until the transfer is complete. I trust you, Sir Douglas, but if the battleship appears I want to be sure that you can signal them to lower its sails. I would not want the battleship to disrupt the save transfer of your wife."

"Agreed," said Sir Douglas. "Captain Shaw signal the boats immediately. Captain Bourne you are a true gentleman. Before I join you on the Freedom I would like you to meet my wife so that we can give her the good news together."

Before rowing back to the Freedom, with Captain Shaw and Sir Douglas as his ``guests``, Captain Bourne made Bill captain of the prize ship. He left two armed sailors to be Bill's bodyguards.

"Have no fear, Bill," said Captain Bourne, "I am quite sure that the battleship will not appear, and you will soon be on your way home."

Bill knew that Pixel had disabled the battleship. "I am not afraid, captain. I agree with you that we will not see that battleship again."

Captain Bourne was right. Some hours later, the transfer of the crew and Sir Douglas's wife was safely completed, and Captain Bourne was relieved and happy to say goodbye to his guests.

"Goodbye, Captain Bourne," said Sir Douglas. "You are a chivalrous American gentleman. You can be sure that I will be reporting this incident in the British parliament when I return to London. I am confident, sir, that your country and mine will soon be at peace."

"That is also my wish," said Captain Bourne.

Bill was now in complete control of the captured trading ship. Captain Bourne transferred a few sailors from the Freedom to help Bill manage the sails and the tiller. Bill's job was simply to follow the Freedom, wherever it sailed. That evening Pixel had his first of many midnight meetings in

Captain Bill's cabin. Bill insisted, happily, that Pixel call him "captain'. He proudly showed Pixel the luxurious bedroom that had been used by Sir Douglas and his wife. He also showed Pixel some wooden furniture that had been made for a child's doll house.

"Look at this tiny rocking chair," said Bill. "Pixel is this the right size for you?"

The rocking chair was on the captain's table which was covered with maps and charts. When Pixel sat in the tiny chair he was face to face with Bill who was sitting in the captain's chair.

"I like it," said Pixel.

"I think Lord Douglas must have had it hand carved in Jamaica for Lady Douglas. She was probably taking it home to their mansion in England for their new baby," Bill explained.

"What does 'Lord' and 'Lady' mean?" asked Pixel. "Those are new words for me."

"Well first of all it means that Lord and Lady Douglas are very rich." said Bill. "In England the people who are very rich are given titles like Lord and Lady. It signifies to commoners, like me, that they are rich, and should be respected. The King and Queen of England have the most important titles. The King also decides who should be called "lord" or "lady.""

"And how does someone become rich?" asked Pixel.

"That's a good question, Pixel. Some people are born rich, they inherit wealth from their parents. Others become rich by creating a profitable business. Some become rich by stealing from other people. Do you not have rich people on your planet?"

"No, we do not have words for "rich" and "poor". I am not sure why we are so different. It could be our size, and the fact that our planet is much smaller than yours. It could be the fact that we learnt how to use the power of the sun."

"The power of the sun?"

"Bill, this ship is powered by the wind. We don't have ships on my planet. Our seas are also much smaller than yours. But if we had needed to move a ship over the sea we would have used the power of the sun. The power of the sun enables everyone on my planet to fly. So we have no need of sailing ships."

'Is the power of the sun used in your flying carriage?"

"Yes, it is used in all machines on my planet. Bill, in the future, I am sure that everyone on your planet will be using the sun's power to fly."

"Pixel, in truth I cannot understand how you can capture the sun's power. But I can tell you that if someone learned how to do that on our planet he would become very rich indeed. Surely the person who developed this magical power must be very rich? Has your planet never had Kings?"

"We have had this knowledge for thousands of years, Bill. For reasons I cannot explain, we have evolved quite differently from the people of Earth. I have much to learn about your planet before I can understand why we are so different. I am not sure whether or not we have had kings in our distant past. I will do some research on the flying carriage to see if there are any ancient stories of kings."

"Research?" asked Bill. "Do you have books in the flying carriage?"

"Not books, Bill, but a device that stores the information contained in many thousands of books. I can search this device for the information I need and display it, just like the images I showed you in Le Havre. One day I will show you a page from one of our books. Our letters are quite different from those in your alphabet. We still have copies of books somewhat like yours. But they are very ancient and are stored in special, protected places. I have never seen one of these ancient books."

"This is very confusing for me, Pixel. We will have to talk a lot more before I can begin to understand your planet."

"I agree. We can talk more later. But I would like you to show me where New York is on this globe. I have flown over all the cities on the American coast. But I don't know their names. If you can name the cities on this globe I will be able to record them on my chart in the flying carriage."

"We may not be going to New York. Captain Bourne told me that we are heading for Charleston in South Carolina. Its closer than New York. He hopes that he can get the prize money for the British ship from American authorities in Charleston. Then he will sail the Freedom to New York. I will have to decide whether or not to ride to Mary from Charleston or sail to New York with Captain Bourne."

Bill showed Pixel where the two cities were located on the globe, and named the other major cities on the Atlantic coast.

"Great," said Pixel. "I will make images of both harbours tomorrow and check for British battleships. I could bring the flying carriage right into the cabin so that you could have a direct look at the images of the harbours."

"Good idea, Pixel. I have told the crew that I will do the midnight watch. I will leave the cabin door open so you can fly in any time after midnight."

When Pixel flew over New York city he was very surprised to find that there were over fifty British battleships in the waters around Manhattan Island. There were no battleships in the Charleston harbour.

"There must be a major battle in New York." said Bill when Pixel gave him the news.

"Captain Bourne is wise to be heading for Charleston. I wish there was some way I could warn him about New York."

"Perhaps there will be news of the battle when you get to Charleston. At the current sailing speed I estimate that it will take about thirty days to get to Charleston."

"And the battle may be over by then. Pixel your daily reports are very useful. I hope the American patriots will have forced the British out of New York by the time we get to Charleston."

For several weeks Pixel had nothing new to report. Bill's role as captain was quite simple, he just had to stay close to the Freedom. There were lively discussions about life on Larth at the midnight meetings in the cabin. Bill shared tales of his life at sea, how he met Mary, and what he hoped to do when he returned to the farm.

"But the truth is, Pixel, that I am not really a good farmer. I sometimes think that Mary and I should have stayed in Boston. I could have learned the trade of blacksmith. Mary has always talked about wanting to be a teacher."

"I don't understand." said Pixel. "Then why did you go that far away to start the farm? Why did you not stay in Boston?"

"It's quite simple, Pixel. Mary had inherited a small sum of money from her father. It was not nearly enough to pay down on a house in Boston, but more than enough to buy land on the frontier. Other young couples were doing the same thing. It seemed right for us. We both worked very hard to clear the land and build the cabin. But I was discontented, I missed the sea. I will work even harder when I get back to the farm."

"But you would be happier doing something else. Bill, that's what I have been trying to explain to you about life on Larth. We only do what makes us happy."

"And you also explained that no one uses money on Larth! How can you be happy without money?"

"We have everything we need without using money. I am trying to understand why money is so important on earth. There are still many things I need to learn before I can understand the role of money on your planet." They were silent for some time. Bill could not understand a world without money.

"What do you plan to do when we get to Charleston?"

"It depends on what happens in the battle for New York." Bill replied. "If we get word that the British have been defeated in New York and Captain Bourne decides to sail there, then I will go with him. New York is a lot closer to the farm than Charleston."

"How will you get to the farm if you decide to leave the ship in Charleston?"

"My plan is to buy a horse and supplies and head north on the coastal roads. Pixel this is where you are going to be a great help. Each night if you can show me your overhead images of the way ahead I will be able to draw a map for myself. It will be more difficult when we have to head west. There will be fewer roads as we get closer to the frontier. I might even buy a rifle for protection. It will be an adventure!"

"I will stay close to you." Pixel said, assuredly.

In their nightly meetings Pixel now sat in his tiny toy rocking chair on the captain's table, with Bill facing him in the captain's chair. It seemed to both men the most natural thing to do.

But Bill did check frequently to ensure that no crew member approached the captain's cabin when Pixel was inside.

One night, a few days before they reached Charleston, Pixel told Bill about his visit to New Orleans, and his encounter with pirates.

"You should have tried to find a treasure map," said Bill with a laugh. "You and I could then go searching for a buried chest of treasure on the beach of a hot tropical island."

"I don't understand," said Pixel.

"It's just a fable, Pixel. No one really knows what pirates do with the money they steal. People make up stories of buried treasure. I was just joking."

On the night before they arrived in Charleston they made plans for meeting near an inn north of the city. Pixel would fly that night to Mary with the good news that Bill had arrived safely.

CHARLESTON

Bill was very frustrated with the horse he had just purchased from the blacksmith in Charleston. They were on a country road just outside the town, and the horse refused to go any further. He had arranged to meet Pixel about twenty miles north of Charleston. Bill had been told that twenty to thirty miles per day would be the normal range for a horse. Of course Pixel had not been told that Bill had never ridden a horse before. Bill did not think it was worth mentioning this detail because he was quite sure that, with a few lessons from the blacksmith, he would soon become a competent rider.

The ride had started well enough. It was a really beautiful spring morning and the horse seemed to be quite content with the way she was being handled by Bill. However after a few miles Bill became quite uncomfortable in the saddle. He discovered that the muscles he used for hauling ropes on the ship were not the ones he needed to ride a horse. Sitting in the saddle became so painful that Bill had to dismount and walk. The horse at first accepted the situation gracefully, and allowed herself to be led by the reins. But then, unaccountably, she stopped. Perhaps she had lost respect for Bill, or perhaps she was much happier trotting than walking. In any event Bill's pulling and tugging on the reins could not budge her, and in disgust Bill sat down, fuming, by the side of the road.

Pixel had flown to the farm the previous night to tell Mary that Bill had landed safely in Charleston. When Pixel arrived back in Charleston, late in the afternoon, Bill was still having a battle of wills with the horse, miles from where they had agreed to meet. When Pixel finally found Bill he was surprised to see him resting by the side of the road.

"Pixel, I am really glad to see you! I think we should change our plan. I think you should fly me to the farm. I have been thinking about it all afternoon. This stubborn mule is just not going to do what I say. I am going to make a better rope swing than the one we had in Le Havre. If we flew two hours or so every night, and I walked during the day, I would make much better time than I would riding a horse. Believe me holding on to the rope swing is much more comfortable than riding horseback!"

Pixel could see that Bill was very angry. "Mary and the children send their love. They are very anxious to see you."

"I'm sorry Pixel. I should have asked about your flight home. I am also anxious to see them. Flying would get us home sooner. What do you think?"

"I don't mind flying at night, but we would have to careful about where we land."

"I thought of that too, Pixel. If we flew from say seven to nine in the evening and landed close to an inn I could walk there and get a place to sleep. I could walk during the day and we could meet somewhere on my route. Every day we can look at the maps in your flying carriage to plan the best route."

"Bill, you know that there are vast forests between the towns on the coast. We may sometimes have to land in the middle of a forest. I know that there are bears in the forest. Are there other animals that we should fear?"

"Yes, and there could be Indians, but I think you would see their tents in your overhead review. Your flying carriage could frighten away any creature we are likely to meet."

"Then I think we should do it. What do we do next?"

"I am going to get on the horse and try to ride to the inn. If I can ignore the pain I may be able to convince her that I am in charge."

The horse had been studiously ignoring the conversation between Bill and Pixel. When Bill approached her with new determination she was quite willing to cooperate. She now seemed to have respect for Bill, perhaps she was just bored and ready for some exercise.

The inn had a bar, a small dining area downstairs, and four guest rooms on the second floor. Pixel was hiding in Bill's hat when he booked a room at the inn. When they were alone in Bill's room Pixel flew out the open window and returned shortly with the spacecraft. He wanted Bill to look directly at the spacecraft's pictures of the planned route.

"I think I will make a quick sketch of the route," said Bill who proceeded to draw a very accurate copy of the image he saw on the spacecraft's monitor.

"That is very well done," said Pixel. "Bill, you are very talented."

"I learned this on my first ship, when I was just a boy. My captain had me make copies of the charts that he had of the ports we visited. Sometimes he would make me amend the charts based on what we actually observed when we visited a particular port. The sea charts available to captains are often inaccurate. Captains need to have charts that are very accurate to avoid collisions with hidden rocks or reefs."

"Well you certainly have a talent." said Pixel.

"Pixel, I have an idea! I just realized that making charts may be just the job I need. I have been feeling very uneasy about going back to work on the farm, I could be a farmer again, but I am not sure that I would be happy. I would enjoy making charts, and if we lived in Boston I know that sea captains would buy them. And, since my charts would be based on the real maps of the harbours that you have in the flying machine, they would be much more accurate than the charts now used by sea captains. What do you think, Pixel?"

"The charts I have seen are certainly not accurate." said Pixel. "I studied the globe in the captain's cabin on the captured ship. It is quite different from the real image of earth that I have in the flying carriage.

I could help you by making accurate images of harbours, you would just have to tell me which ones were needed. Would this make Mary happy?"

"I think so. I think she would be happy to get a job as a teacher in Boston. She knows that I am not a good farmer."

"So what do you plan to do?"

"It's just an idea, Pixel. I don't have a plan. Money would be the problem. I would first have to sell the farm. That might take time."

"Money, Bill? I have never seen money. Could you show me some money?"

"Pixel, you still have not explained to me how you get by without money on your planet. Here is a silver coin that is worth one dollar. And here is a one dollar bill in paper form. This is money that we use to buy food, clothes, horses, anything we need. I plan to use some of this money to buy one or two cows when I get to the farm. It is my share of the money that Captain Bourne received when he gave the captured ship to the American government in Charleston."

"That's not enough money for you to move to Boston?"

"It would help, but it would not be enough. I have to think about this some more, Pixel. Mary might have other ideas. Right now I should just focus on getting home. Tomorrow I am going to try to sell the horse, and find a carpenter to help me with the new rope swing. I think I will have to spend another night in this inn."

"I will do more research on our route and try to find alternative inns that you might want to stay in. I will meet you here tomorrow night."

When Pixel visited Bill the next evening the floor of the room was covered with rope, blankets, a rope swing with a carefully crafted wooden seat, and other camping supplies.

"I want to be prepared in case I have to sleep outside." said Bill. "It could still be wintry when we get further north. I sold the horse so now I will have to be hiking with quite a lot of supplies."

"We could leave the rope swing attached to the flying carriage." Pixel suggested.

"Yes we could. But then you would not be able to meet with me in the inn. The windows in an inn will not be large enough for your ship with the rope swing attached. I have a new plan that I would like to try tonight. I think I can fly all through the night on this new rope swing. In the morning you can put me down close to a farmer's field where I will sleep for a few hours and then start walking to the nearest inn to get a meal, and food and water for the flight. Instead of sleeping in an inn I will sleep in a field somewhere during the afternoon. Pixel you can be close by all the time, with the rope swing attached to the flying machine. What do you think?"

"We can try," said Pixel. "But when I am flying with you I will land every hour to make sure that you are all right."

That first night Pixel flew with Bill over farms, forests and small towns in South Carolina. They travelled for over one hundred miles. If anyone saw them that night they probably thought they were looking at an unusual type of witch. But Bill was not bothered by such thoughts. Before sunrise Pixel had landed him by the side of a crude dirt road that led to a small town. Bill slept on the ground, wrapped in blankets, until noon. He then hiked into town and had a sumptuous lunch at the local inn. After lunch he walked the route that he had mapped out from Pixel's images, and Pixel met him later that afternoon. After a short nap he was ready for his next night flight.

By the morning of the seventh day, Bill was only one day's walking distance from the farm. "I will fly ahead and tell Mary that you will be home tonight," said Pixel. "But Bill, I won't be there when you arrive. There is something I want to do before I see you and Mary together."

"What do you mean Pixel? Where are you going? What do you plan to do?"

"I am not sure, Bill. It may take some time, but I will be back. I will tell you then."

"Pixel I am sure it must be important to you. We will miss you. Will you tell Mary and the children?"

"Yes I will, Bill. I will tell them that you will be home tonight and that I will be away for a few weeks."

THE PIRATE

Don Sebastian was a very unusual pirate. Since he never went out on blood curdling pirate expeditions, perhaps he should not really be called a pirate. But he was deeply involved with pirates; he was the leader of a group of pirates who operated out of the bayous of the Mississippi river where it flowed into the Gulf of Mexico. Don Sebastian lived in the city of New Orleans. He was the part owner of a company that handled the cargo of ships coming to, and going from, New Orleans.

He was born in Spain, and like Bill, had been an orphan who ran away to sea. He was only thirteen when the Spanish ship he was sailing on was boarded by pirates, just outside New Orleans. When the pirate captain learned that Don could read, and was an orphan, he decided to take Don back to his pirate's lair in the bayou. The pirate captain wanted Don to teach him to read. The pirate captain never did learn to read; Don read everything for him. The captain began treating him like his own son. When Don was sixteen the captain allowed him to go to New Orleans on his own to learn about life in the city. Don was entranced by the bustling, exciting city. When he returned to the bayou he convinced the captain to let him get a job with a shipping company. They discussed how this might lead to Don getting information about ships leaving New Orleans. The captain could use this information to target specific ships that sailed from New Orleans.

The pirates profited from the cunning scheme; they respected the captain for his courage and leadership and Don for his intelligence. When the captain was murdered in a silly dispute with a hot headed young pirate, Don rushed to the bayou to assume control. He knew that he would be challenged by the young pirate and his friends. But Don realized that most of the pirates would support him and he had also learned from the captain, who he considered his adoptive father, that decisive action was essential in a pirate leader. When he was confronted by the young pirate and his rebel friends Don casually removed his hat, and bowed respectfully to the young pirate. On rising from his elaborate bow, Don revealed that he had a small pistol hidden in his hat. Without a word he shot the young rebel through the chest. He died immediately. The rebel's friends were shocked. They had not expected that this bookish man, stylishly dressed and bespectacled, could be so brutal. It was quite clear to all the pirates that Don Sebastian was their new leader.

When Pixel explored the pirates' camp, he knew nothing of Don Sebastian. Pixel was trying to find where the pirates' treasure was buried. He believed that there might be some truth in Bill's stories about pirates. It was also an opportunity not to be with the family for Bill's homecoming. Pixel felt that he might be a distraction in the family when Bill returned home. He wanted Bill to have the pleasure of being with his family again, without a tiny alien from another planet getting in the way.

Pixel had been at the camp for over a week; he had seen no sign of buried treasure, and neither had he seen Don Sebastian. The pirate's ship, hidden in a mangrove swamp, had not been to sea during that time, until the day a messenger arrived with news from Don Sebastian that a suitable cargo ship was leaving New Orleans that very night. It was suitable because the cargo included a large shipment of Spanish gold and silver coins, and because the ship was unarmed and unescorted.

Pixel watched as the pirate ship was towed hurriedly out of the mangroves by several rowboats. When the ship was in open waters the pirate captain had the sails hoisted and they headed out to sea to wait for the Spanish prize.

The Spanish ship was detected around noon on the next day and was soon captured by the pirates. The Spanish captain at first denied that there was treasure on board his ship. "We have only coffee and tobacco!" he pleaded.

"Senor, if you force us to search the ship and we find gold and silver then I will be very angry with you," said the pirate captain. "And I will have to kill you! But if you give me the treasure that I am so politely requesting then you will be free to take your coffee and tobacco to the good people in Spain."

Not surprisingly, the Spanish captain accepted the pirate captain's proposal and the gold and silver was quickly transferred to the pirate ship.

It was night when the pirate ship returned to the mangroves. Pixel was hiding in the captain's cabin where the treasure was stored. He wanted to know exactly how the treasure was shared and, if Bill's stories were true, where it was buried. But when the pirate captain went to sleep in his bunk, Pixel realized that there would be no treasure buried that night. He spent the night in the spacecraft that he had parked in a tree, high above the enormous alligators that prowled the swamp. They were the fiercest creatures that Pixel had ever seen.

The treasure was not divided until Don Sebastian arrived the next morning with one of his trusted bodyguards. On the main deck, with the captain and the crew gathered around, Don Sebastian counted the treasure and gave each pirate their agreed share. Don Sebastian had been taught by his adoptive father that, to ensure the loyalty of the pirate crew, it was very important that the division of treasure should be fair and open.

Pixel was amazed at the rousing party that erupted when Don Sebastian had given the last pirate his share of the treasure. The captain had barrels of rum brought to the main deck so that the crew could toast Don Sebastian. "Bravo, Senor Don!" they shouted.

Don Sebastian joined in the celebration. He drank rum with the crew and warmly congratulated every pirate. Before he left the party he had a final message for the crew. "I must return to New Orleans to work for you," he said. "You men may have a holiday, but I must work diligently so that we can have more celebrations, and soon."

"Work hard, Senor Don!" they shouted as he was rowed away into the swamp by his bodyguard.

Don Sebastian did not go directly to New Orleans. He was rowed instead to a tiny island, deep within the bayou; an island he had discovered when he was growing up as a teenager. He had built a cabin on stilts then, and used it as his personal library. The library contained many of the books that his pirate father had seized from prize ships. It was now a much bigger and more sturdy cabin. It still had many of his old books, but they were slowly disintegrating because of the very hot, humid conditions in the swamp. It also contained several metal boxes filled with gold and silver coins. Don Sebastian's treasure chests.

Don Sebastian was greeted by an older pirate who guarded the treasure with the help of two angry dogs. He was one of two pirates who guarded the treasure; they both lived with their families in New Orleans, but they took turns, every other week, camping out in a dry area close to the treasure island. Pixel watched as Don Sebastian was rowed out to the island. He saw him climb the short ladder and enter the cabin with a bag of coins.

When he was being rowed away Don Sebastian said goodbye to the guard. "Good day, Miguel, and be watchful. You must visit me next week when you return to New Orleans."

"Thank you, Senor Don. It would be a great honour," replied the guard, very respectfully.

Pixel was very pleased. Bill's stories were true, there was buried treasure! But not buried in the ground. This was going to be a lot easier for Pixel than he had imagined.

Pixel watched Miguel for several days before he took action. At midnight he flew the spacecraft into the cabin and parked it on a pile of books. Then he used his laser gun to slice into the side of one of the treasure chests. It took some time but he was not worried because Miguel and the dogs were sleeping soundly on the shore opposite to the island. A large piece of the side of the chest fell to the cabin floor when he drilled the last hole. Gold and silver coins gushed from the chest to the cabin floor.

Pixel parked the spacecraft on top of the pile of coins. Two woollen bags, attached to the iron ring, rested on top of the coins. Pixel now drove the all-terrain vehicle from the body of the spacecraft and started loading coins, one by one, into the bags. It was the first real test of the all terrain vehicle. It had a front loading device which could grip and lift coins into the bags, but it slipped constantly on the shifting coins, and it was very awkward for Pixel to load the coins in the bags. To solve the problem he decided to cut the cover from one of the old books and then used the all-terrain vehicle to move the cover to the pile of coins. By re-arranging some coins he created a flat area in the pile, and he was able to manoeuvre the book cover into a position where it became a solid base for the all-terrain vehicle; it was easier to load the coins.

Outside the cabin the two dogs were getting agitated. They had been bemused by the sound of the falling coins; they paced anxiously on shore, beside the sleeping guard. They growled softly, unsure of the new sounds coming from the cabin.

"What's the matter?" Miguel asked, sleepily. He shined his lantern on the cabin. "There is no one there," he said to the dogs. "Go back to sleep."

The dogs growled more loudly. "Alright, I'll have a look." said Miguel angrily. He searched the shore for alligators before pushing his boat into the swamp. "Damnation!" he shouted when he had paddled a few yards into the swamp. When Pixel looked out the window he saw Miguel rowing frantically back to shore. The laser holes in the bottom of the boat had proved to be a prudent measure.

It took several weeks for Pixel to return to the farm. He had to fly slowly to avoid the bags being blown from the spacecraft. He flew close to the tree tops so that he could land quickly if the winds became strong. When the winds were turbulent he took shelter in caves or on cliffs. But mostly he simply landed on the floor of the forest and anchored his ship by a tree.

It was evening time when he flew into the candlelit cabin.

"Pixel is back!" Sally shouted.

"We have been so worried about you, we thought you were killed!'

"Where have you been Pixel? Tell us of your adventures! We are so happy to see you again!"

Pixel was quite overwhelmed with the joyous greetings. "Mary, could I bring in the flying machine? I have a present for the family."

"Of course Pixel, we have all been wondering about your surprise," said Mary.

The family was astonished when Pixel landed the flying machine on the kitchen table, with two bags of gold and silver coins attached!

Mary was shocked. "Where did you get these coins? Pixel did you steal this money? How could you do such a thing!"

Pixel was surprised and hurt. He had nothing to say. He believed that giving the family money would make them happy. All the discussions he had with Bill had convinced him that moving back to Boston would make the family happier.

"This is all my fault, Mary," said Bill. "You should not be angry with Pixel, you should be angry with me. I talked to Pixel about by idea of starting a business in Boston, and I talked about the need for money to start the business. We had countless hours together on the captured British ship.

We became very good friends, and we talked as friends. I think we should let Pixel tell us how he got these coins. Pixel just wanted to make you happy. That is what his kind feel compelled to do. All the people on his planet are like that."

"I am very sorry, Pixel," said Mary. She could see how unhappy he had become. "Please tell us your story."

"Perhaps I should just take the money back," said Pixel. He was very sad and confused. He had imagined the delight that Adam and Sally would have had when he told the story of his adventures. He was not sure that he even wanted to tell the story now, perhaps he should fly away and try to meet another family.

"Please tell us your story, Pixel," said Adam. "Now I know why you wanted me to attach the bags to the iron ring. I want to know exactly how you got the coins into the bags."

"Yes Pixel!" said Sally. "We want to hear your story."

"You would make us all very happy if you would tell us your story." said Mary, tenderly.

So Pixel narrated his adventures with the pirates with many interruptions from Adam and Sally, a few whispers of 'oh my' from Mary, and several approving shouts of 'well done' from Bill.

When the story was finished Pixel said, 'I will return the treasure immediately."

ARTHUR HUGHES

"Pixel," said Bill, "I would have done exactly what you did if I had your special skills and if I was as brave and as resourceful as you are. You remind me of my favourite hero—Robin Hood! Just like you he robbed from the rich to give to the poor. What do you think now, Mary?"

"I think that Pixel is a greater hero than Robin Hood. And I think that we should start planning for our move to Boston," said Mary.

"Hooray for Pixel!" shouted Sally and Adam.

Mary reached out her finger to Pixel. He knew that they were friends again.

And this time Pixel did allow Sally to stroke his hair.

BOSTON

The house that Bill and Mary bought in Boston had once been owned by an eccentric, retired sea captain. It was built exactly as he had imagined it during the years he spent at sea. The house was located on a rocky beach close to the Boston harbour where ships from all continents were moored. The sea captain had designed a deck, located outside the attic of the house, which looked out to sea. He had binoculars installed on swivels so that he could track the ships entering and leaving Boston harbour. He used signal flags to send welcoming messages to the ships' captains. Often he would know the captain and they would communicate with flags. Over the years it became the normal practise for ships entering the harbour to send a signal of hello to the retired captain. The attic behind the captain's deck contained the charts and mementoes that he had accumulated from all the foreign ports he had visited. The only access to the attic was by a rope ladder, through an opening in the attic floor. The captain's wife complained that the ladder was designed to keep her out. She was a rather plump woman and very good natured. She was quite happy that her husband had what she called 'his private ship's quarters, upstairs!'

The first thing that Mary did was have Bill replace the rope ladder with regular wooden stairs. The attic became Pixel's home, Bill's drafting office, and a play room for Adam and Sally.

Most evenings Pixel would fly into the attic and park the spacecraft on a platform right beside Bill's drafting table. Bill would study the overhead image of a harbour on the spacecraft's video monitor and draw a chart of the harbour. He would then have copies of his charts printed for sale to sea captains. It proved to be a very profitable business for Bill. Not only did the charts show an accurate outline of the harbour they also showed hidden rocks. Pixel had designed the video images to highlight, in color, any rocks below the level of the sea. The sea captains were so impressed with Bill's charts that they recommended them wherever they sailed.

Mary got the teaching job she wanted and, for the first time, Adam and Sally got to go to a regular school.

Pixel became very interested in the American war for independence. He knew that some time in the future Larthans would have to make contact with government leaders on Earth. If Larthans could share their knowledge with Earth scientists it would help the people of Earth to improve their standard of living. But with so many nations at war on Earth this was certainly not the time to approach any Earth government. Pixel would not do this in any event without specific instructions from Mission Control. In the meantime Pixel would learn as much about governments on Earth as he could.

Mary would buy the weekly Boston newspaper and a special reading easel was set up so that Pixel could read what was happening in the war. Bill and Mary would discuss the news with him so that he really understood what he was reading in the newspaper. Mary also borrowed history books from the library for Pixel. He read endlessly. He finally read, and understood, 'Robinson Crusoe'.

It was in these nightly discussions with Mary and Bill that Pixel learned that the war between the American colonies and Great Britain was about freedom and democracy. He learned that America was trying to become the only country in the world that was not ruled by a king or an emperor. From the Boston library Mary was able to get a copy of the Declaration of Independence that announced to the world, in July 1776, that Americans were free to set their own destiny. That they would no longer be ruled by the King of England. When Pixel read the opening statement which said in part that "everyone had an unalienable right to Life, Liberty and the pursuit of Happiness" he realized that the American dream was very much like life on his own planet. Pixel wanted to visit the battlefields where the war was being fought, but Mary asked him to promise never to do that. "A stray bullet could kill you instantly!" she said. And Bill agreed.

Over the next five years Pixel spent most of his time trying to learn how the new American government would manage the war and its new freedoms. The new government met in Philadelphia, and Pixel attended many of their sessions. He was fascinated with their discussions about a constitution for the new country. He also flew to England, to the parliament in London, to hear them debate their war with America. One day he flew to the King's palace and observed a meeting that the King had with the Prime Minister of England.

Pixel discussed everything he learned with Bill and Mary in the sea captain's attic. Mary became so knowledgeable about foreign affairs that she suggested to Bill that they start their own newspaper. Bill had already bought a printing press that he used to print his charts so it was quite easy to start printing a weekly one page newspaper devoted to foreign news. Mary wrote the editorials.

In 1783 their newspaper was the first to report the news that the war was over. At a peace conference held in Paris, Britain had accepted that America was an independent country. Pixel had attended the conference and flew back to Boston with the news.

Later that year a second spacecraft from Larth arrived on Earth. It was a much larger, better equipped ship than Pixel's. It had five Larthans on board, two couples and a young woman named Tamra. Pixel had been anticipating the spaceship's arrival for some time. He was excited and anxious to meet his own kind again. He was looking forward to teaching them all that he knew of their new home.

LARTH

When Mission Control received Pixel's first messages from Earth, three years after they had been sent by Pixel, they were immediately transmitted over the Larthan internet. Since every room, in every house on Larth had an internet monitor, everyone on Larth was transfixed with the images from Earth and terrified for Pixel when they saw that the intelligent life forms were giants! Mission Control transmitted the images at the same time every evening so that Larthans could plan their day accordingly. No one wanted to miss the nightly broadcasts. When they started to receive images of the pages from the novel 'Robinson Crusoe' Larthans set up individual study groups to try to translate the words into Larthan. Children started speaking like Adam and Sally without understanding a word that they said. Pixel was everyone's hero. All of the images that Pixel sent were stored on the array of computers that serviced the Larthan internet, and therefore were available, at any time, for viewing by Larthans. The English language was being studied not just by linguists, but by everyone on Larth.

The Larthan internet was quite different from the internet we have on Earth. It was hundreds of years older than our internet, and much more advanced. Internet monitors were the sole means of communication on

Larth. There were no Larthan telephones, no cell phones, and no radios. There were internet monitors in public places, somewhat like the pay telephones that we have on our planet, but of course they were free to all Larthans. The internet was solar powered, wireless, and voice activated.

Skilfully designed robots were used to manufacture, operate and distribute almost everything that Larthans needed to live comfortably. And everything was free. There was no need for money on Larth. Because robots did all the boring, repetitive work Larthans had time to pursue creative, interesting careers. Thousands worked in the space program; as computer programmers, scientists, engineers and, of course, as designers of robots.

Money was not needed on Larth because no one owned anything to sell. It was impossible for Pixel to explain this to Bill. The concept of 'ownership' did not exist on Larth. The resources of the planet—the land, the robots, the buildings, the technology—were owned collectively by all Larthans. They understood, inherently, that the resources of the planet were to be used to make all Larthans happy. Larthans were motivated to share, not to compete.

There are only two continents on Larth, and just one relatively shallow sea. People on Pixel's continent were a light shade of green, the people on the other continent were a light shade of purple. There had never been a war between the two peoples, they shared the same technologies and the same internet system.

Gardening was the only work that did not involve robots. Larthans were vegetarians; they were passionate about growing their own food. They shared any surplus food that they grew. Vegetable kiosks were distributed throughout Larth, like the always open convenience stores in most large cities on Earth. Larthans would deposit their surplus vegetables in their local kiosk for anyone to use. Although they would never admit it, Larthans were very competitive in trying to make their gardens as beautiful as possible. They really thought that making their garden pleasant to look at was a way to make their neighbours happy.

Larth had no army, no police, no jails and no government. Larthans painted, wrote novels and engaged in sports. They produced movies, but they did not have the fierce intensity that we are used to on Earth. The images that Pixel sent of his experiences with giants on Earth were more engrossing to Larthans than anyone on Earth could possibly imagine. The result was that thousands of Larthans volunteered to go on the second mission to Earth.

The chosen astronauts met with Mission Control to plan what they would do when they arrived on Earth. When Mission Control learned that they would be dealing with giants on Earth they had to decide what special tools should be taken. Should they have weapons of some sort? Should they try to make contact with other giants?

The new spacecraft included six single person airplanes, one for each of the five astronauts, and one for Pixel. The spacecraft had all the tools and equipment that would be needed to build a permanent home base on Earth.

Each of the five astronauts had a variety of skills, and each contributed to the selection of tools and equipment that would be taken. Tamra was the only astronaut with medical skills and she took great care in selecting, and in some cases, redesigning the medical equipment needed. She also suggested, and helped to create, a special camouflage for one of the airplanes. Working with artists, sculptors and engineers she designed the aircraft so that it looked like an eagle; just like the pictures that Pixel had sent to Mission Control. The wings were retractable to reduce wind resistance when the plane was travelling at high speed.

Mission Control had a farewell party for the astronauts and of course Pixel's parents were there to wish them well, and to send love to their son. Tamra was quite tearful when she met Pixel's parents and she hugged Pixel's mother for a long time. Tamra's parents were also there, they came from the purple continent. They told Pixel's parents how much they admired their son's bravery, and how much he was idealized by Tamra.

After the party Pixel's mother said to her husband, "I like Tamra. I hope Pixel likes her too."

"She is quite beautiful. I have always thought that women from the purple continent were more beautiful than women from our continent," her husband said, jokingly. "But, you my dear, you are the exception! I am sure Pixel will like her. But will she like Pixel?"

CORSICA

───◄◆►───

Pixel chose the island of Corsica as the Larthan home base because it was close to the countries that Mary thought were the most advanced in the world: Great Britain, France, Spain and Holland. The spacecraft landed in a meadow high in the rugged mountains, remote from the Corsican families who lived in small farms in the coastal lowlands.

Pixel had been in direct contact with the astronauts for several months, he knew their names and their backgrounds. All of the astronauts were skilled linguists. Thern, the husband of Budra, knew all of the eighteen Larthan languages. It was Thern who asked Pixel to give them lessons in English; months before they landed on Earth. So when the astronauts exited, groggily, from the spacecraft, Pixel could greet them in English, "Welcome to Earth!"

Thern ran forward, and exactly as he had seen in Pixel's videos from Earth, he solemnly shook Pixel's hand. "Greetings from Larth, Mr. Pixel! Your homeland has best wishes for her favourite hero!"

The five Larthans surrounded and hugged Pixel. They bombarded him with greetings, love from his parents, special notes from his friends, and news about Larth. All of this spoken in the Larthan language.

Pixel responded in Larthan, a little haltingly because he had not used the language for so long. He was immediately interrupted by Budra. She was by far the happiest and most playful of the five astronauts. It was her good humour that often reduced stress during the boring, but sometimes dangerous space flight. She was an expert in robotics and had been very involved in the design of the robotic tools that would be used on Earth. But now she just wanted to have fun. "Pixel, I think that Thern will have to give you three months training in the Larthan language before we can begin to understand you." she laughed.

Xento, who was an expert in the robotic mining equipment used on Larth, had to defend Pixel. "I think Budra is wrong." he said. "Pixel, I am sure I can teach you to speak Larthan in less than one week."

But Xento's wife, Greida, whose expertise was in botany, had the last word. "I am sure that Xento will be able to teach you, Pixel, but I will have to give him a few lessons first." Everyone laughed. They all wanted to try flying, and they urged Pixel to take them on a tour of the island. They were delighted with how smoothly they were able to soar in their gravity controlled suits.

Pixel was introduced to the new tools that they had brought to set up a permanent home base on Earth. They agreed with Pixel that Corsica was an ideal location. They found a cave, on a high cliff close to where they landed, that they could convert into a suitable home base.

The cave was big enough to hold the spacecraft, which was quite large, about the size of a pickup truck. Living quarters could be built inside the cave and there was ample room for all the tools and robotic equipment that they had brought from Larth. But they all opted to live outside the cave in their own homes that they would build for themselves. The living quarters in the cave would be used only in an emergency.

Pixel decided to live in the spacecraft, he still visited with Bill and Mary at least once a week. He still considered Boston his home on Earth. The spacecraft would be used for meetings or for study. It had a large computer with all the technical data that was available on Larth.

Since the spacecraft was solar powered it had to be parked outside the cave for several hours a day to keep its solar batteries fully charged. Xento, the mining expert, built a door at the cave opening that could be lowered like the drawbridge in an ancient castle. Budra programmed the drawbridge to open and close at designated times so that the spacecraft could automatically fly in and out of the cave.

The spacecraft was really a mobile construction machine with multiple tools. It had a laser that could slice and loosen large rocks, and a robotic, mobile lifting mechanism that could carry rocks or other materials for great distances. Xento used the spacecraft's tools to make the door to the cave from local rocks. It was cleverly designed to blend with the surrounding rocks and terrain. It was unlikely that a Corsican could ever detect the cave opening because only a highly skilled mountain climber could scale the cliffs below the cave.

Tamra decided to build her house in the crook of a tree, high enough that she had a wonderful view of the Mediterranean Sea. It was just large enough for a bedroom and a large living room. Except for her bed, which came from the spacecraft, she made all the furniture from twigs that she found on the forest floor.

The first two months were spent improving their English. Apart from trips to Boston, Pixel spent all his time teaching the new arrivals. They mastered English very quickly and Pixel was anxious for them to start learning other languages. Pixel thought that they should each try to find a human mentor to teach them a language, as he had done with Mary and her family. The other Larthans agreed with this approach, but they had misgivings.

"I want to agree with you, Pixel." said Thern. "But you must admit that there was a great deal of luck involved. You were certainly very courageous, but you would not have talked to Mary if you had not seen how desperately she needed help."

"I was very afraid." said Pixel. "But when I saw Mary sobbing, hopelessly, I thought of my own mother. And, in my eyes, Mary was no longer a giant, she was just a mother who needed help."

"I completely understand," said Thern. "I wish I could say that I would have the courage that you showed that day. But it is very unlikely that we will get such an opportunity. We will have to approach the giants directly, somehow gain their trust, convince them to help us, and keep everything they have learned about us a secret, even from their closest friends."

"It will not be easy, Thern." Pixel replied. "I know that. You may have to try meeting several giants before you find someone you can trust. Mary tells me that some giants do believe in small creatures called faeries, but most logical thinking humans think faeries are a myth. If you approached a giant and decided that he could not be trusted, you would just have to fly away. The giant would have no way of proving his story. He might not even tell the story to his friends, he may be afraid that he would be consider a foolish believer in children's fables. And remember Thern, earthlings do not have an advanced communications system, there would not be any widespread distribution of stories about aliens from another planet."

"I agree with Pixel." said Tamra. "There is so much poverty on Earth, and so much conflict that I think it will be easy to find mentors, especially if we can help them in some way. I agree that we should not tell our mentors that we are from another planet. I think that would alarm them. Since they have a folklore that recognizes beings called 'fairies' I think we should let them think what they will of us. Sometime in the future, when their society is more advanced, we can reveal that we are from another planet, but for now I think we should be wary of sharing the truth with the giants."

"Tamra makes good sense." said Thern. "I am willing to accept your approach, Pixel. But we should be realistic and realize that we may not be nearly as successful as you have been."

"I think we should try Pixel's plan," said Budra. "We can meet at least weekly to discuss the progress we are making. We can share ideas and learn from each other."

It was finally agreed that Thern and Budra would try to find a mentor in Holland who could teach them Dutch, Xento and Greida would look for a mentor in Spain, and Pixel would help Tamra to find a French mentor.

"Would you like to come to Le Havre with me tomorrow Tamra?" Pixel asked. "I can introduce you to the French couple that Bill met, when he and I arrived in France. You may find them to be good mentors. They were certainly very friendly with Bill."

Tamra hesitated for a moment, and then she said, "Of course Pixel, if that is what you would like."

"I think you will enjoy meeting them," said Pixel. "We can head out right after breakfast tomorrow."

They were an odd couple in flight. Pixel in his new, sleek plane, and Tamra in 'the Eagle'. It was the name that Pixel had given to Tamra's plane, even though he doubted that a plane camouflaged as an eagle would be practical. But Tamra had convinced him, in several flight demonstrations, that the Eagle could be very useful in some situations. So this morning he was very happy to be crossing the Mediterranean Sea, flying side by side with the Eagle, for an adventure at Le Havre.

When they arrived at the woods close to Pierre's farm they parked their airplanes and then flew to the beach where Pixel had dragged the escape boat ashore.

"Bill was very cold and shivering when we arrived at this beach," Pixel told Tamra. "I had to find a farm as quickly as possible. I will show you the farm now. I assume that Pierre sold the boat to the fishermen further up the coast."

When they flew into the barn Marie was milking one of the cows. "They make cheese from the milk," said Pixel. "Tamra, cheese is delicious! There is no food like it on Larth. If you do become a friend of Marie and Pierre, and they offer cheese to you, I suggest you give it a try. I am sure you will like it."

Since Pierre was busy in the fields Pixel took Tamra for a tour inside the couple's house.

"This is the kitchen where the couple spend their evenings. I think that after supper would be a good time for you to make contact. We have time to visit the prison in England where Bill was held prisoner, and I can show you London, the capital of Great Britain."

Tamra was very quiet when they returned later that evening to the barn.

"I think this would be a good time to meet with Pierre and Marie," said Pixel. "Are you ready to try, Tamra?"

"I'm ready," replied Tamra, and she flew immediately into the couple's kitchen.

Marie was knitting and Pierre was sitting in a kitchen chair smoking a pipe when they heard a tiny voice, *"Parlez vous anglais?"*

They both stood up, startled, and stepped away from the kitchen table. Tamra looked at them defiantly.

"Its' a devil!" shouted Marie, (in French, of course). "A purple devil!' said Pierre fearfully.

Tamra did not understand what they said, but she was quite angry when she flew out of the kitchen and met with Pixel in the barn.

"What happened?" asked Pixel who was surprised that Tamra had spent such a short time with the couple. He could see that she was very annoyed.

"I don't know how to tell you this, Pixel. You have a good plan and I would like to make you happy. But I am not ready for your plan. I dreamed of exploring this planet with the same freedom that you had when you first landed here. Pixel, I need some time to do that. I am leaving you now. Please tell the others that I will be away for some time. I will be travelling east to see the other continents."

Pixel was shocked. "Tamra, I did not know that this is what you wanted."

"I know, Pixel. You never asked me."

THE VIKING WAY

━━ ⊨◈⊨ ━━

Pixel flew to Boston right after Tamra left him for her round the world tour. Mary had been scolding him, in jest, about his long absences. The family knew that Pixel was busy with his compatriots in Corsica; they had shared his excitement in the weeks leading up to the arrival of the spacecraft. Mary had teased him that he was now more interested in Tamra than his first family in Boston.

When a disconsolate Pixel described Tamra's sudden departure the family immediately did what they could to console him.

"It's not your fault, Pixel," said Sally, who was now fourteen, and very confident. "I can understand Tamra wanting to go on a world tour. She was cooped up in that space ship for months and months. She's young, she just wants an adventure."

"Sally's right," said Mary. "Just think of your adventures when you first arrived on Earth. No one was telling you what to do."

"I never told Tamra what to do," Pixel protested. "Everything was decided by consensus; that's the Larthan way."

"Pixel, you have told us that Larthans are free to do what makes them happy," said Mary. "Tamra just wants to be free."

"I am glad Tamra is off touring the world," said Adam. "Pixel, perhaps you will have time now to help me get to Paris."

"Paris?" Pixel was surprised. "When did you decide to go to Paris?"

"It was a family decision, a family consensus," said Mary, laughing. "Seriously, Pixel, we have decided that we could use a news reporter in Paris. The plan would be for Adam to go to Paris, learn French, and prepare written reports that you could bring to Boston. You would be our reporter in London and Adam would be our reporter in Paris. Our newspaper will be more interesting if we can print news from both countries."

"That makes good sense." said Pixel. "How can I help?'

"I would like you to fly me there with your flying carriage." said Adam.

"Fly across the Atlantic on the swing! That's impossible Adam. It would take days. You couldn't hold on that long. If we encountered a storm . . . ." Pixel was perplexed.

"That was exactly my reaction, Pixel." said Bill. "But Adam has an interesting plan. I think you will be impressed. Adam I think you should tell Pixel about the Vikings."

"Pixel," said Adam. "I am sure you know more about Vikings than I do. You were always passionate about learning history. I found it boring. But a Norwegian friend told me a Viking story that I had never heard before. Pixel can you tell me when America was discovered by Europeans?"

"You mean when it was discovered by Columbus? 1492. America was discovered in 1492." Pixel replied.

"My friend thinks that the Vikings discovered America five hundred years before Columbus. His grandfather told him a story about Vikings who sailed west from Greenland to a new country they called Vinland. He believes that Vinland is Newfoundland, the British colony north of Nova Scotia."

"That's interesting," said Pixel. "But what does that have to do with your flying across the Atlantic?"

"Let's look at the globe," Adam replied. "Greenland lies about 600 miles due north of Newfoundland. That's the distance that the Vikings rowed to get to Vinland. Iceland is about three hundred miles east of Greenland. The Vikings had settlers in Greenland and Iceland hundreds of years before Columbus discovered America. As you can see Iceland is about 600 miles from Scotland. My idea is that we take the Viking route to Europe. We would fly overland to Newfoundland and then over the sea to Greenland. After crossing Greenland we would fly to Iceland and then to Scotland. The longest flight over water would be 600 miles, about eight hours of flying time."

Pixel was thoughtful. "It is very cold in Greenland. Could you hold on to the ropes for eight hours in very cold weather?"

"I have invented a new swing." Adam replied. "We can look at it outside. It looks like a hammock, but it has a light wooden frame that I think will make it quite stable in flight."

"Adam will be sleeping most of the way," Bill laughed.

"I will be sleeping sometimes," said Adam seriously. "But Pixel that means we would be flying most of the time; we could land every eight hours or so for me to a stretch and walk around. I think we could get to Scotland in about seven days. I would carry water, food and blankets in the hammock."

"And some gold coins." Mary added. "We think Adam should abandon the hammock in Scotland in the highlands west of Aberdeen and then travel by stagecoach to London. He will need funds for board and travel in England and France. Pixel this is a good time to thank you for all that you have done for us. The businesses that you helped us to start are very profitable. Without your help we could not have dreamed of such an adventure for Adam."

Kind words from Mary always made Pixel cry. He hid his tears. "Thank you Mary. This adventure will make me happy. Adam, I think I would like to have a look at your hammock."

"We can do a practise run in the woods tonight." Adam suggested.

"It will be like old times." said Pixel, thoughtfully. He tried not to worry about Tamra; this adventure with Adam would be good therapy.

TAMRA

When Pixel's father told his wife that the women from the purple continent were more beautiful than the women of the green continent, he was of course just teasing her. The women from both Larthan continents were all beautiful. But most Larthans would agree that the women from Tamra's continent were just a bit more adventurous than the women on the green continent. And for a good reason. The purple continent was more mountainous and rugged than the green continent. It was a continent with white water rapids, towering waterfalls, and jungles teaming with exotic wild life. The purple Larthans lived closer to the natural world than the green Larthans; they had more time for adventures in the wilderness.

Tamra's mother and father were both doctors so it was natural that she chose to study medicine. Doctors on Larth were focused primarily on accident related injuries. Broken arms or legs resulting from accidents in the wilderness areas were the kind of injuries most often dealt with in Larthan hospitals. Larthans were very healthy, they lived in a pollution free environment. For minor ailments Larthans consulted the internet.

Tamra was only fourteen when she joined the space program. She made a promise to herself that she would one day join Pixel on Earth.

When the first images of the giants were received on Larth her passionate desire to join Pixel was intensified.

She was now quite confused in her feeling towards Pixel. She admired his rational thinking, and mostly agreed with the actions he proposed for interacting with the giants. But in her mind he seemed to have lost the desire to explore the rest of the planet, he seemed obsessed with politics. There was no rational explanation for her decision to fly off on her own. At least none that she thought that Pixel would understand. She just wanted to be free to explore the wonders of Earth.

When she left Pixel at Le Havre Tamra flew directly to their home base in Corsica. She gathered supplies for her trip and flew south-east to the North African coast. She had no plan. She would fly east and explore any city that seemed interesting to her.

By nightfall she had reached Egypt and was soon entranced by the pyramids. She used the x-ray machine on the Eagle to view inside one of the pyramids and detected the shaft leading to the pharaoh's tomb. She wondered how such an enormous structure could have been created without the benefit of solar powered machines. She imagined the thousands of slaves that would be used, just to bury a king! That night she slept on top of the pyramid while the Eagle circled above in a brilliant desert sky.

In the morning she saw a caravan of camels heading into the desert. She flew to the back of the last camel in the caravan and found a comfortable perch. She removed her solar power pack so that she could lie down on a bundle of cloth. She enjoyed the gentle sway of the camel ride, but by midday it was so hot that she considered landing the Eagle so that she could fly away in its air-conditioned cabin. But she saw date palms and water in the distance and she knew that the caravan would soon be reaching an oasis.

The oasis was quite large and Tamra found a secluded area, far from the camels quenching their thirst, where she could find water for herself. The pool she found was so isolated that she decided that it would be safe enough to have a swim. She hid her solar power pack under a date tree, and dived into the refreshingly cool waters. This was the kind of adventure that she was longing for!

In the evening the camel drivers had a communal meal in a large tent. Tamra watched them from outside the tent, there was nowhere to hide in the noisy crowd. She followed one of the camel drivers to his own small tent. He sat down on the sand in front of his tent and contemplated the stars in the desert sky. Tamra thought this would be a good opportunity to talk to a giant.

"Good evening," said Tamra when she flew to the ground just in front of the camel driver.

The camel driver was startled, a tiny purple creature speaking a strange language! But he quickly realized that the creature was a jinni and that he should be very careful what he said to him. He knew that the jinni had the power to grant wishes to ordinary humans. The 'jinni' of course is the 'genie' we know so well in the story of Aladdin and his magical oil lamp. The camel driver had heard many stories of jinn who had done bad things to humans. So he was very friendly and respectful when he said to Tamra, in Arabic, "How can I help you Jinni? I would like to help you Jinni."

Tamra was surprised by the tone of the response. She had not expected such a calm and peaceful reply. She did not understand the words, but it was clear that this giant wanted to be a friend, She wondered whether the word "jinni" was comparable to the word "faerie."

"Me, jinni?" she said, pointing to herself.

"Jinni." said the camel driver, not wanting to disagree with Tamra.

Tamra was not sure what to say. These giants believed in something called a jinni, and it seemed that Larthans could be easily mistaken for jinni. If she had time perhaps she could build rapport with this giant, but in the morning he would be leading his six camels across the desert. There was never going to be time to have a meaningful discussion. Tamra was encouraged by the encounter, but it was time to say good-bye.

"Jinni go now," said Tamra, and she flew away quickly to rendezvous with the Eagle.

The camel driver was very relieved to see her go.

In the Eagle Tamra had to decide where she should seek her next adventure. Pixel had developed a computerized map of Earth that showed all the cities and places that he had visited, or that he had learned about from maps that Bill owned. Tamra and the others had downloaded this global map into the computers in their airplanes. Tamra reviewed this map as the Eagle flew due east towards India. Pixel had also shared with his compatriots everything that he knew about the political situation in Europe and the wars, and reasons for wars, between the European countries. She set a course for Bombay in India, a country that Pixel said Great Britain was fighting to control.

When she circled Bombay in the morning she could see that the harbour was filled with many trading ships and several British warships. She landed the Eagle on a remote hill overlooking the city. Since she planned to spend some time in the city she parked the Eagle in a crude 'nest' and flew down to the harbour. She discovered that the British authorities were located in a castle close to the docks, protected on the seaward side by numerous cannons.

She explored the exotic town outside the castle. It was magical. Tamra was awed by the towering elephants that worked meekly for the giants, carrying huge loads of cargo to the trading ships in the harbour. She saw giants sitting cross-legged on the ground playing a flute like musical instrument and seeming to control the movement of giant snakes. The snakes appeared slowly out of baskets, swayed by the snake charmers who somehow soothed them with a tune of the flute.

She saw bazaars filled with beautifully coloured cotton and silk fabrics. She explored store rooms fragrant with spices.

She spent weeks exploring the villages, farms and jungle inland from Bombay. She stayed away from the monkeys who lived in the city. They seemed to be very aware of her and would try to grab her if they were close enough. She discovered the ornate palace of an Indian prince. One day she followed the prince as he went on an expedition into the jungle, riding in a festive carriage on the back of an elephant. When she flew to the carriage, to get her first ride on an elephant, she discovered that the Prince had a guest, an Englishman.

Indian peasants were beating the jungle brush ahead of the elephant to try and force a tiger into the open. Tamra did not know this but she had joined a tiger hunting expedition. She realized this when the prince pointed excitedly to a tiger that was crouching in long grass, just in front of the elephant.

"There you are, Jim. There is your shot!" said the prince.

Tamra saw the Englishman raise his rifle and aim directly at the tiger. Tamra had learned about guns from Pixel. She had seen British soldiers target shooting in the castle grounds in Bombay. She did not want the tiger to die! Instinctively she flew to the barrel of the gun, right in the face of the Englishman, and shouted, "Don't shoot!"

It was too late. Jim had pulled the trigger and the explosion sent Tamra reeling backwards.

"What was that?" shouted the prince.

"A purple faerie!" said Jim. "Unbelievable. Did you not see it Prince Lanni?"

"I saw something. But it flew into the forest." said the prince.

Tamra recovered quickly and was pleased to see that the tiger had disappeared. But she was not happy with herself. She realized that her action could have resulted in the death of one of the beaters. Pixel would not have reacted in such an irrational manner.

When she returned to Bombay she flew immediately to her favourite garden. It was a beautifully maintained garden with a cool arbour covered with flowering vines. Tamra loved to hide in the arbour and watch a young English mother play with her two small children. The young mother was the wife of a colonel in the British Army. The English mother had a visitor, an Indian lady, who was reading a book in her native language, Hindu, and translating the words into English. Tamra had no intention of learning an Indian language, she did not intend to stay long in India, but there was no harm in learning a few words.

When the lesson ended, Tamra followed the Indian teacher, whose name was Vanatha, as she walked down a dirt path to her home in the city. She stopped at a shrine at the roadside and said a silent prayer. When she started walking again Tamra saw that she was crying. Tamra had meant to talk to the teacher when she reached her house. She was intent on making contact with giants whenever she thought that a good conversation was possible.

"Vanatha, why are you crying," asked Tamra who had flown to a tree branch just in front of the teacher.

Vanatha did not seem surprised to see Tamra. "Have you come to help me?" she asked.

"Do you know who I am?" asked Tamra.

"I think so," said Vanatha. "I just prayed for help and you appeared. Can you help me?"

"Perhaps I can. Can you tell me what help you need?"

Vanatha was perplexed. "I am surprised that you are speaking in English. I prayed for strength to deal with the ordeal tomorrow."

"Tell me about the ordeal. Maybe I can help."

"I thought you would know," said Vanatha. "My sister is going to die tomorrow. I prayed for courage. I cannot bear to think of her death."

"Is she sick?" asked Tamra. "How do you know she will die?"

Vanatha started crying again. She had prayed to an Indian god and now she was talking to a tiny purple girl, speaking English! "My sister will be burned alive tomorrow, with her dead husband. It is sati!"

Tamra was horrified. "Burned alive! Why? Why do you allow this?"

"It is the custom in our community. It is sati! I may not agree with it but I am powerless to stop it. It would bring shame to my family. I prayed for courage. You are not helping me. You do not know sati. Perhaps you should leave me with my sorrow."

"Does the English lady you are teaching know about this? I don't think that this is an English custom."

"The English have nothing to do with our customs. I have not told the English lady."

"Why does your sister not just run away?"

"I told you! It would bring shame to the family. She can't run away. Please leave me now!" And Vanatha ran crying down the pathway.

Tamra was very perplexed. What would Pixel do in such a situation? Why should she be concerned about this one death when wars and killings, Pixel had told her, had always been part of the growth of civilization on this planet. And what could she do, anyway? She spent a restless night in the Eagle pondering her dilemma.

On the next day, towards evening, Tamra watched the funeral procession wend its way towards the river. Relatives of the dead Indian pulled a wooden cart, filled with firewood, through the narrow streets. The dead husband, finely clothed, was laid out in the firewood. His young widow, overcome with fear, crouched beside him. Male relatives of her husband stayed close to the cart as it was drawn through the crowds. They wanted to ensure that the widow did not try to escape from the bier.

When the funeral pyre reached the river the procession halted and solemn words were read. The pyre was lit with a flaming torch. At that moment the Eagle, which had been circling overhead on auto pilot, dove towards the crowd at tremendous speed! The plane buzzed above the crowd, circling around and around the funeral pyre.

"The gods are angry!" someone shouted. Everyone ran away in panic from the burning pyre, and the angry eagle.

Tamra flew to the widow who was still on the pyre, petrified, as the flames rushed towards her.

"Follow me!" shouted Tamra in Hindu. "Follow the red cloth!"

Tamra had tied a long, thin strip of cloth around her waist. It fluttered in the wind like the tail of a kite.

"Follow the red cloth!"

Vanatha was also close to the flaming cart. When the crowd fled she ran towards her sister. She heard Tamra urging her sister to leave the pyre. "Follow the red cloth. You can trust the English faerie," she shouted, as she pulled her sister from the fire.

The sisters ran after Tamra who flew above the crowd, the red cloth streaming behind her. When they had escaped from the crowd Tamra turned into a quiet lane and slowed down so that the sisters could walk at a normal pace. Vanatha realized that the purple faerie was taking them to the home of her English student.

Tamra did not stop to explain. She kept going until they reached the garden gate. The English mother, her name was Tabatha, was waiting on the veranda. She ran to the gate as soon as she saw her daughter's favourite ribbon floating up the hill, followed by Vanatha and her sister.

"Your plan worked!" she said excitedly to Tamra. "What a clever faerie you are. Welcome Vanatha. And this is your sister. Adrika, I am so glad to meet you. Let's go inside, we can have cake and tea on the veranda. Adrika, you will be safe with us. We will help you in any way we can."

Vanatha spoke to her sister in Hindu and Adrika smiled and bowed gracefully to Tabatha.

"Adrika cannot speak English," said Vanatha. "But she is very grateful to you and the English faerie for saving her life. She cannot return to her family. She will do anything that you suggest. Tabatha, this is so kind of you. I was afraid to ask for your help. Your English faerie has magical powers."

"She is not my faerie, but she is magical. She alone is responsible for rescuing your sister. You should thank her."

"Tabatha I have to leave you now," said Tamra. She had untied the string which held the ribbon around her waist. Tabatha's daughter, Amanda, had been delighted to lend her ribbon to the English faerie. "Please thank Amanda for loaning me her ribbon. Please tell her I will do my very best to visit her when she returns to England. And thank you Tabatha. You have been so kind."

"I know Tamra. You must complete your quest. I hope you keep your promise to visit us in England. The children will be expecting you. You are a wonderful faerie. Good-by Tamra."

"Good-by Tabatha. I hope I can see you again."

Tamra was very happy as she flew back to the Eagle. She was astonished at how readily and gracefully she had been accepted by Tabatha. Tabatha's five year old daughter, Amanda, had seen Tamra as soon as she landed on the patio table that morning. "Look mother!" she said. "A faerie!"

When Tamra shouted "Please help me!" Tabatha immediately said "It's an English faerie, children, we must help her!"

It had been so easy, then, to discuss her problem with Tabatha. Tamra was reluctant to tell the grim story in front of the children so she told Tabatha that it was a secret story that only she could hear. When Tamra saw how disappointed the children were when their mother took them to the veranda to play she immediately promised to visit them in England, when she had finished her secret quest. As soon as she heard Tamra's story Tabatha agreed to help in any way she could.

Tamra wished she could stay with Tabatha and build the kind of relationship that Pixel had with his 'family' in Boston. She was touched by the kindness of this gentle giant. But she was also lonely. She wanted to share her story with Pixel, and with Thern, Budra, Xento and Greida.

When she had the Eagle in flight she fell into a deep sleep. The plane was heading due east. She had not yet decided where to go. She was too confused to make any plans.

She was awake very early and her global map showed that she was not far from Mount Everest. This would be her chance to view, up close, the mountains that had looked so majestic during their orbits of Earth. The Eagle struggled to reach the peak of the mountain, the plane had not been designed for such a height. And it was bitterly cold in the cabin. Tamra spent only a few moments at the peak before taking the Eagle down to the foothills, to a Tibetan monastery built on the side of a mountain. The sound of bells ringing led her to a room inside the monastery where monks were chanting lyrical hymns. She was sure that a young monk, just a boy, saw her as she hid behind a huge bell. He smiled at her, but continued chanting with his elders.

Tamra was now very anxious to return home to Corsica. She was quite ready to find a French mentor. She hoped that she and Pixel could be friends. But first she had to complete her childhood dream of flying all the way around this marvellous planet.

She followed the Great Wall of China to Beijing, the capital city, the biggest city in the world. It was also the most mysterious city in the world. Within the city the Chinese Emperors had built a walled compound for their palace and government offices. It was called the Forbidden City. Tamra spent a week exploring the palaces. She saw rooms filled with scholars writing documents in the intricate Chinese script, so unlike the English alphabet and her own Larthan letters. She was baffled by the elaborate ceremonies that were held whenever anyone met with the Emperor. She watched an extraordinary meeting where foreign visitors had to kowtow to the Emperor before they were allowed to offer him gifts. They had to kneel and touch their foreheads to the floor, nine times!

Tamra's next stop was the palace of the Japanese Emperor in Tokyo. She was dazzled by the samurai warriors practising martial arts in the courtyard.

In Hawaii she found the gardens of the natives not unlike her own garden on Larth—wild and filled with beautiful flowers.

When she crossed the Rocky Mountains in southern California she discovered a band of Indians, on horseback, hunting a herd of bison. She rode precariously on the back of one horse and watched the rider use a bow and arrow to shoot down a bison.

She flew to New Orleans and used Pixel's map to find Don Sebastian's secret treasure hut in the bayou. All she found was Don Sebastian's books decaying in the remains of the hut, the treasure had been looted by other pirates.

The final stop on her round the world tour was the sugar rich island of Jamaica. She was horrified to discover that the workers in the sugar cane fields were slaves. She was more than ready to fly home, ready for the long flight across the Atlantic ocean.

When she was in radio range she contacted Xento and Greida in Spain, and they immediately radioed the news to Thurn and Budra in Holland, and to Pixel who was in London, listening to political speeches in Parliament. They agreed to meet with Tamra at the home base. They had no news from her for over three months; they were very anxious to see her.

VERSAILLES

Xento and Greida had spent a week exploring Barcelona before they decided on a strategy for meeting a giant who would help them learn to speak Spanish. They felt that an elderly couple would be the most likely to help; they would have more time and patience than a young couple. If they were lonely an elderly couple might enjoy the companionship of Larthans. They followed an elderly gentleman who they saw limping home from a nearby store. Inside the house they saw him handing a newspaper to his wife who was confined to a wheelchair. After watching the couple for several days Xento and Greida decided to approach them.

In those days most newspapers were just a single page. When Xento found out where the newspaper was printed he and Greida stole a copy. They simply tied a piece of string to a hole they made in the newspaper and Xento flew with it to the couple's home. The couple were having breakfast when Xento landed on the kitchen table, with the newspaper, and shouted the only Spanish words he knew, *"Buenos dias, Manuel. Buenos dias, Catalina."*

The couple were quite surprised, but pleasantly so, especially when the Larthans started projecting video images of Barcelona on the kitchen wall. Catalina was captivated by the show and Manuel was delighted to see his wife so happy. He knew a few English words and somehow understood that the tiny creatures wanted to learn Spanish. When Xento and Greida returned the next morning with another newspaper and more videos it was clear to Manuel that the tiny students were going to be regular guests. That same afternoon he limped downtown to buy an English-Spanish dictionary. The two hour walk was nothing to him when he thought of his wife's delight with the tiny students.

In Amsterdam, Thern and Budra had encouraged two elderly sisters to teach them Dutch. The sisters were widows of two sailors who were lost at sea. Some of the widows' neighbours said the husbands were not lost, they had simply decided to stay away from their cranky wives. The sisters liked to argue, but Budra was such a happy person that she soon found ways to make the sisters laugh, and they competed with each other in trying to be the best teacher. In a few weeks their neighbours were pleasantly surprised by the transformation of the grouchy sisters—they were now bubbling with happiness!

Thern was also learning French, once a week, from an elderly bachelor in Marseilles. The bachelor had an extensive library and did not believe for a minute that Thern was an English fairy. He was prepared to teach Thern the French language but he was quite persistent in questioning Thern about England. Since Thern was unable to adequately answer his questions the bachelor was convinced that Thern was from a tiny, remote island in the Pacific Ocean.

Budra preferred to stay in Corsica and study the farmers there, rather than learn another language with Thern. She became very interested in wine making. She concocted a grape drink that she decided she would serve at the homecoming party for Tamra. That was her first thought when she got the radio message that Tamra was coming home.

It was a wonderful homecoming! Tamra had so many stories to tell, so many videos to show, and they had so many questions.

Pixel was quietly delighted to see Tamra. During Tamra's world tour Budra and Greida had several long meetings with Pixel to help him overcome his discontent. He felt that he had been inconsiderate to Tamra, he felt very guilty for not asking her what she wanted to do. He had been so focused on language training that he had not ever considered that she might want to be free to explore the planet, just as he had done. Budra and Greida were very light hearted in dealing with Pixel. They assured him he would always be a hero to Tamra, that Tamra was probably equally concerned that she had offended Pixel. Watching Tamra now Pixel realized that Budra and Greida were right. There was no hint from Tamra that she was in any way disillusioned with Pixel. She was most affectionate and caring.

The next morning everyone met for breakfast in the cave. Tamra had been very attentive to the stories the couples told about their language instructors. She was ready to learn French.

"Pixel, would you help me find a French instructor? I think I am ready now. Please forgive me for being so foolhardy."

"Tamra I would love to help you. But you don't need my help. You have the courage and creativity to do anything you want. You will find someone in your own way. And you can call me if you ever need me."

"I could help you get started on French," said Thern. "I am developing a French/English dictionary on our computer. You and I could meet each evening and I could coach you. I would introduce you to my instructor in Marseilles but it would just give him a chance to ask even more questions."

"Thanks Thern," said Tamra. "I can start today. And Pixel, I will be asking for your help. I am not sure where in France I should start."

"My suggestion would be Versailles," said Pixel." It is the home of the King of France. It is considered to be the most beautiful, the most magnificent palace in Europe. And from the speeches I hear in the British parliament it is a place of intrigue. You could learn a lot there. Since England and France are still at war with each other you and I could be learning exactly what each country is saying about each other. I am still trying to understand why there are so many wars on this world. Earth is so rich in water and land and other resources. I think everyone on the planet could have healthy prosperous lives, if they could just learn to live in peace."

"Pixel, I am not an expert on Larthan history but I think we also had conflicts in our distant past. Once humans develop the same level of technology that we have they may very well learn to live in peace."

"I hope so."

"I am sure they will, Pixel. I will visit Versailles. But I will be calling you if I need help."

"I suggest we meet in Paris," said Pixel. "As you know Adam is now living there and trying to gather news for the family newspaper in Boston. I see him every week; we could meet in his apartment."

Before Tamra left for Versailles Pixel encouraged her to come to England with him to see the British parliament in operation and also the King of England's palace. He wanted her to understand the difference between the role of the King of England and the role of the King of France.

"You have talked a lot about parliament," said Tamra. 'But I am not sure I really understand the importance of parliament. What exactly is parliament?"

"Parliament is a special group of men who meet to debate important problems facing the country. When they reach a consensus they recommend a solution to the king. The men in the group are elected by ordinary English citizens. So, theoretically, they represent the wishes of all Englishmen. The king usually accepts the solutions proposed by parliament, and passes a law to make it happen. France does not have a parliament, the king makes all the decisions himself. I am not sure how the French King makes these decisions. You might learn more about this when you explore Versailles."

"Parliament is somewhat like our system," said Tamra. "Larthans are voting every day on proposals made by other Larhans."

"You are right, Tamra, there is a comparison between the two systems. When they develop the technology that we have perhaps they will change their parliamentary system. We could not have developed our voting system if we had not developed the means to communicate with everyone, instantaneously. Everyone on Larth is part of a worldwide parliament. That's why we no longer have a government on Larth."

"I will try to find out what I can when I get to Versailles. But I have to be honest, Pixel, I am more interested in finding out what their doctors know about medicine."

The next few months were very busy ones for Tamra. She spent three days each week at Versailles, one day a week with Pixel and Adam in Paris, and the rest of the week in Spain or Holland with the other Larthans. She studied French every night with Thern in the computer room on the spacecraft.

Tamra soon understood why the palace at Versailles was considered the most beautiful in Europe. The immense gardens were immaculately and tastefully groomed. When she parked the Eagle and viewed the palace buildings from ground level she was awed by their beauty, and their size. It was going to take her a long time to explore these buildings.

After a few days she realized that most of the buildings at Versailles were simply apartments for the king's nobles. The wives of the nobles seemed to spend most of the day getting dressed in elaborate costumes. They all wore towering head-dresses that were so precariously balanced that ladies had to walk very slowly, and very carefully. It seemed to be a waste of time to Tamra. Life in the palace seemed to be contrived and unreal.

The king's kitchen was actually Tamra's favourite place at Versailles. The variety of food, the creative excitable chefs, and the organized bedlam of cooking was more real to her than the pretentious behaviour of the nobles and their wives.

But there was magic at Versailles. Elaborate picnics in the gardens, with jugglers and clowns. Plays in the king's opera house. Boating on the artificial lakes. Glittering dances in the palace ballroom. Versailles was a vast entertainment park designed to please the nobles and their families.

The king's bedroom was the biggest surprise for Tamra.

"I think the king's bedroom is the French version of parliament." Tamra told Pixel when she was met with him in Paris.

"What do you mean?" asked Pixel.

"Every morning there is a meeting of all the nobles in a large conference room, just outside the king's bedroom. It is not an organized meeting like the parliament in London, the French nobles are standing around in small groups, talking loudly and with great passion. They are trying to get the attention of two nobles who are obviously the king's prime ministers. When the king has finished his breakfast the two prime ministers join him to discuss what they have heard from the nobles. My French is not good enough to understand anything that the prime ministers report to the king, but what they say seems to be very important to the king. The king is a very quiet man, I think he agrees with whatever the prime ministers suggest."

"They were probably discussing taxes," Pixel assured Tamra. "From what I hear in the English parliament it seems that the French king is trying to raise taxes to pay for the French army which is apparently the largest army in Europe. His ministers are trying to tax the nobles, but the nobles think the French peasants should pay the tax. Since the French peasants are too poor to pay more taxes the king has a very difficult problem. The French government may become bankrupt because of the greedy nobles."

A few days later Tamra was surprised to see almost a hundred nobles on horses gathered near the king's stable. They were all dressed in scarlet coats and the king was leading them at a slow trot towards the forest that extended from two sides of the palace gardens. The king was following twelve hounds who were held in leash by an elegantly dressed trainer. When the hunting dogs reached the forest they were released, and they began sniffing in the bushes for the scent of fox. Suddenly one of the dogs started yelping loudly and dashed through the forest in chase of the fox. The others dogs followed quickly and the king and the nobles crashed through the forest in pursuit. It reminded Tamra of the buffalo hunt with Indians in America, but more dangerous. The nobles had to ride their horses at breakneck speed, avoiding trees, leaping ditches and changing direction quickly as the dogs zigzagged through the under-brush. Tamra saw one horse trip and fall as it tried to leap over a small stream. The noble remounted quickly and was back in the chase.

The forest was the king's hunting preserve. Over the years his ancestors had bought land from local farmers to enlarge the hunting area. But a few peasants still owned small farms within the forest. The hunting party skirted a peasant's cottage and managed to avoid the adjoining garden. But a noble who had fallen behind in the chase decided to take a shortcut by riding directly through the garden, quite close to the cottage. At that moment a young girl was running from behind the cottage to see what damage had been caused by the main hunting party. She tried to stop as soon as she saw the horse, but it was too late! The rear leg of the horse struck her in the head and she fell to the ground. The rider did not stop. He may not have realized that someone was hurt. Tamra was horrified. She flew quickly to the girl who was lying unconscious in the garden. Tamra did not know what to do. She could hear the sound of the hunting dogs getting fainter as they pursued their quarry deeper into the forest. Tamra was alone with the girl. She needed help from Pixel. She sent an emergency radio signal to the Eagle that would be transmitted automatically to the other Larthan airplanes. It was a distress signal that would urge Pixel and the other Larthans to fly to the Eagle, as quickly as possible.

Tamra flew over the cottage to see if any of the hunters might be returning to help the girl. And then she saw a young man running towards the cottage. He was shouting, "Sylvie! Sylvie!" as he ran towards the girl. Tamra watched the young man pick up the girl and lay her gently on her bed in the cottage. He knelt by her bedside and sobbed as he gently stroked her forehead.

Tamra flew to a small table at the head of the bed and shouted, "I can help Sylvie! I am a doctor."

She wanted to say the words in French, but she was too nervous to remember the right words.

"An English speaking fairy?" The young man was astounded. "A doctor?"

"Yes, a doctor." Tamra replied, surprised but pleased that he was speaking English.

"A fairy doctor?" the young man was mystified. He didn't believe in fairies, but he was talking to a tiny purple creature with wings!

Tamra wanted to avoid talking about fairies. "What is your name, young man? My name is Tamra."

"My name is David. I can't believe I am talking to a fairy!"

"David, the most important thing right now is Sylvie." said Tamra gently. "With your help I can save her life. Do you want to help me save Sylvie's life?"

"Of course I want to save her life. I am responsible for her accident."

"What do you mean? How are you responsible?"

"I was running towards the cottage when I saw the hunters ride past her garden. She was in the garden behind the cottage. I was happy to see that she was safe. I called out to her and when she saw me she ran from behind the cottage right into the hunter who had cut through her garden. If I had not called out to her she would not have had the accident. I ran towards the horseman to try and get him to stop but he veered away from me. I ran after him but it was no use."

Tamra did not know what to say. David was now sobbing on the floor beside Sylvie's bed.

After a long while David looked up to Tamra and said, "You said you could save Sylvie, what can you do? How can I help?"

"Well the first thing you can do is cover Sylvie with a warm blanket. And then I suggest you warm some of the soup I see on the stove. If she regains consciousness you may have to give her food. Would you like me to help you start the fire?"

"What do you mean?" asked David.

"Let me show you, David." Tamra directed her tiny ray gun at wood in the fireplace until it burst into flames. "Will that help you, David?"

"Black magic!" David exclaimed. "Are you a witch?"

"Not magic, David, I just wanted to show you that I have tools that can save Sylvie's life. The doctors at the palace do not have the tools that I have. I am not a witch or a fairy. Will you trust me David?"

"I will trust you Tamra. What are you going to do?"

"I have some friends who will be coming to help me. While we are waiting could you tell me what you know about Sylvie?"

"I met her just four weeks ago. I was walking through the forest when I saw her working in her garden. Her father has gone to Paris so she was quite glad to have someone to talk to. Her mother died last year. I have been visiting Sylvie whenever I can. When I saw the hunters ride off from the palace this morning I was worried for her and ran here to see if I could help."

"Why did her father leave her alone? When will he be coming back?"

"I don't think she knows. The crops have been very bad for the last two years and her father had to borrow money from one of the nobles at the palace. The noble threatened her father with eviction if he did not repay the loan. Her grandparents, her mother's parents, have a small bakery in Paris. Her father is hoping that the grandparents can help him to pay the loan."

"How old are you, David? And how old is Sylvie?"

"I'm fifteen, and she's fourteen."

"Where did you learn to speak English?"

"I am English. My father is the head gardener for the King of France."

"David, I need you to help me in a very special way."

"I will do anything to help Sylvie get better. What do you want me to do?"

"My friends are going to be afraid to meet you. They will be upset with me for talking to you. We are not supposed to talk to humans. I want you to promise me that you will never tell anyone about us."

"I will do anything to save Sylvie's life."

"This is very important to us, David. You will see some very unusual things in the next few days. If you keep it a secret and Sylvie gets better I may be able to help both of you in the future. If you tell anyone about us my friends and I will fly away and we will never be seen again. Will you make the promise never to tell anyone about us?"

"I promise never to tell anyone!" said David.

"I am leaving now to meet my friends. I will be back soon."

"What should I do with Sylvie?"

"Just watch her. Talk to her and ask her questions. Ask her to move her fingers. She may hear you and try to respond. I will be back soon."

Budra was waiting for her on the tree branch where the Eagle was parked.

"Hi, Budra, how did you get here so quickly?"

"I was in my plane on the way to Thern in Marseilles when I got your message. I flew here as quickly as possible. How can I help. What is the problem?"

"A young girl has had an accident and I want to save her life. But I need everyone's help and consent."

"Our consent?"

"Yes, let me tell you what happened, Budra."

Budra was very thoughtful when Tamra finished her story. Finally she said, "I understand completely why you would want to help Sylvie. I imagine that Pixel felt exactly the same way when he offered to help Mary rescue her children. We would not be speaking English if he had not made that decision. But I don't see how you can possibly help Sylvie. Do you have a plan Tamra?"

"I have a plan, but it is very risky. That's why I need everyone's consent, and help."

Budra smiled. "You can count on my help, Tamra. I am sure your plan will be an adventure for all of us!"

"Thanks Budra. It will be an adventure. But right now I want to check on Sylvie. Could you wait here and tell the others my story when they arrive?"

"I'll wait here. Good luck, Tamra."

David was still kneeling beside Sylvie when Tamra returned to the cottage.

ARTHUR HUGHES

"Has she made any signs that she has heard you?" Tamra asked.

"No movements at all. Are you sure you can get her better? Have your friends arrived?"

"I think I can. I am still waiting for one of my friends. I want you to meet him. David could you tell me anymore about Sylvie's father? We may need to speak to him."

"I have never met him. But Sylvie did show me a letter that she received from him. I think there is an address on the envelope."

"That may help my friends find him in Paris. Please try to find the letter. Can you read French?"

"Yes, I can."

"That's good. David I suggest you read the letter. It might tell us when her father plans to return. I am going now to see if my friends have arrived."

"I am very worried about Sylvie. Will your friends be here soon? I think I should tell someone at the palace."

"I understand, David. Why should you believe me? I know it seems improbable to you but I am a doctor. I can save Sylvie's life. The doctors at the palace cannot help Sylvie. I think there is a good chance that I can help Sylvie. I really want to help her. My friends will be here soon, perhaps in less than an hour. Please wait a little longer and meet my friend."

"I will wait, Tamra. But I am very worried."

202

When Tamra returned to the Eagle she was greeted by Xento and Greida who had just arrived from Barcelona.

"We will help in any way we can," said Xento. "Budra has told us your story."

"How is Sylvie?" asked Greida.

"There is no change in her condition. I am worried about David. He is very anxious about Sylvie and he thinks that he should go to the palace to get help. I asked him to wait for an hour. I hope that Pixel and Thern arrive soon."

"Don't worry, Tamra," said Budra. "They will be here shortly. I was in radio contact with each of them a few minutes ago. Do you want to go and wait with David? I could fly to the cottage when they arrive and give you a signal, discretely."

"Thanks, Budra. I think I should wait here. David may ask questions that I would not feel comfortable answering. I need a consensus on my plan before I meet with him again."

Budra was right. Pixel and Thern arrived shortly and Tamra told them her story.

"I agree we should try to help Sylvie," said Pixel. "But how? What do you want to do, Tamra?"

"I want to take Sylvie to Corsica. We have imaging equipment in our home base that can scan inside Sylvie's brain. We will have to take hundreds of pictures, but we developed a computer program on Larth that will merge the pictures, seamlessly, so they can be viewed on a monitor. I will be able to view the area inside Sylvie's brain that is swollen. I believe I will be able to detect precisely the nature and location of the injury. I may be able to surgically repair the damage."

"I helped to write that program, Pixel," said Budra. "I never thought we would ever use it. One of the medical experts on Larth suggested that if we could get a brain scan of a sleeping giant it could be compared to a Larthan's brain. Most of us thought it was a silly idea but we developed the program anyway. We never thought it could be used to save a human's life! But Tamra how could we possibly get Sylvie to Corsica?"

"We could use the spacecraft. We have all watched Xento use the spacecraft to clear huge rocks in our cave when he built our home base. I think the spacecraft could carry Sylvie, in her bed, to Corsica. What do you think, Xento?"

"The spacecraft is powerful enough to carry a human," Xento replied. "The bed could be attached to the undercarriage of the spacecraft. But I am not sure about carrying Sylvie in her bed. We would have to restrain her somehow to prevent her from slipping out of the bed while the spacecraft was in flight. And it would be a disaster if she became conscious while we were in the air."

"I thought of that," said Tamra. "I think we could use rope to tie Sylvie to the bed. Our rope is tiny but very strong. We would have to encircle the bed with hundreds of loops but I am sure it would be enough to keep

Sylvie from falling. I would have David tuck her in securely with blankets before we started looping the ropes around the bed."

"Tamra did you think of bringing your medical equipment to the cottage, instead of taking Sylvie to Corsica?" Pixel asked.

"I did, Pixel. The problem is that I am not sure that I can complete the operation in one night. I may need one or two days to monitor Sylvie's recovery, I may need to do more surgery. The spacecraft would have to be located outside the cottage to provide power for the medical equipment. Anyone riding near the cottage would see the spacecraft."

"I understand," said Pixel. "We will have to tell David that Sylvie will be taken away. Is that a problem, Tamra?"

"Yes, Pixel, that will be difficult. If everyone agrees that this plan is worthwhile I would like to introduce you to David. I will explain to him that we will be taking Sylvie away. I will tell him that you will be bringing him a report tomorrow morning of Sylvie's progress. Pixel, you can be the judge as to whether or not we should trust him with our secret."

"I like your plan, Tamra," said Pixel. "I am ready to meet David. Is everyone else ready?"

"I am ready," said Xento. "Tamra, when can I look at the bed and the cottage?"

"I could fly to Paris and get Adam to help us find Sylvie's father." said Thern. "But I will need the address from David."

"I will do anything you wish, Tamra." said Budra.

ARTHUR HUGHES

"So will I." said Greida.

Tamra was very pleased with their support. "Thank you all. I know this is dangerous. We have a lot of details to work out. But first I want to introduce Pixel to David. We have to convince David that he can trust us to remove Sylvie from the cottage. David has to return to the palace in a few hours, his father will be expecting him to be home for supper. When David leaves the cottage we can all meet there and finalize our plan. In our planes we are only an hour's flying time from Corsica, we could bring the spacecraft here late tonight and take Sylvie to Corsica before midnight. I will start my tests as soon as we get Sylvie to the cave. The surgical operation could be completed by dawn tomorrow. So we might be able to have Sylvie back in the cottage tomorrow night."

"We will wait outside until David leaves," said Greida. "Good luck Tamra!"

David was sitting at the kitchen table when Tamra and Pixel flew into the cottage.

"David, I would like you to meet my friend Pixel. We have a plan for helping Sylvie. We will tell you as much as we can about our plan. But first you should talk to Pixel. I told him that you promised not to tell anyone about us."

"Hello David," said Pixel. 'I am sure that you are bewildered by what is happening. I can only repeat what Tamra has already told you, we have the power to save Sylvie's life. But we will need your help. Is that the letter from Sylvie's father?"

"Yes it is." said David, picking up a letter that was on the kitchen table. "I have read it. It explains why Sylvie's father has not returned from Paris. Sylvie's grandfather is very sick and can no longer do the baking. The grandmother is teaching Rene, Sylvie's father, how to bake so that she can keep the bake shop open. The letter also warns Sylvie about Count Avide, the noble who is demanding that his loan be repaid."

Pixel was curious, "Do you know Count Avide?"

"No, I only know a few nobles. I mean I know their names. Nobles don't have anything to do with commoners like my father and me."

"Tamra, I think you should tell David what we plan to do."

"David, we will be taking Sylvie to a special place tonight where we have the tools to make her well. We hope to bring her back to the cottage tomorrow night, but we may have to keep her for one more night. Pixel will coming to the cottage early tomorrow with news about Sylvie. He will be with you all day if necessary. Some of my friends will be trying to find Sylvie's father in Paris."

"Taking Sylvie away? Can I ask how you will do that?"

"You will have to trust us, David. We really have unusual powers. When Sylvie is better and we have time we will tell you more. When do you have to return to the palace?"

"I should be leaving soon, my father and I have supper in the King's kitchen at about six o'clock. He will be expecting me."

"It will be cool outside when we move Sylvie tonight," said Tamra. "David I would like you to tuck the blanket snugly around her so that she does not get a chill in the night air. As soon as you go my friends will be getting ready to move Sylvie."

"And I will be here to meet with you in the morning," said Pixel.

"I feel very guilty, leaving Sylvie."

"Trust us, David," said Tamra.

When David left the cottage, very reluctantly, Pixel and Tamra were quickly joined by the other Larthans who had been waiting outside.

"Quick thinking, Pixel!" said Xento when he flew through the cottage door and took a quick look at Sylvie's bed. "I am glad you asked David to leave the door open when he left. Otherwise I would have had to cut a hole in the door to get the bed out of the cottage. Once the bed is outside I can use the spacecraft to lift it and take it to the cave. Your plan will work, Tamra."

Thern was quite excited. "Did you get the address in Paris? Adam and I could start looking for Sylvie's father early in the morning."

"Yes, Thern," said Tamra "The letter is on the kitchen table. The father's name is Rene. We can talk about him while Xento is flying to Corsica to get the spacecraft. Xento, do you need any of us to come with you to Corsica?"

"No, I will be fine alone, Tamra. I will bring back rope and an all-terrain tractor to move the bed outside. Is there anything else that we might need?"

"Yes there is," said Tamra. 'We have a small problem. Sylvie will have to be fed intravenously. Greida, I know you have been studying the plants in Corsica. Do you think you could create a nutrient rich liquid, from those plants, that would be safe for Sylvie?"

"I am sure I could," said Greida. "For a start I could use the grape drink that Budra likes so much. I would just need to add some essential nutrients to make it a complete food. We will need to make several barrels of the liquid."

"I would like to help," said Budra.

"I will need your help," said Greida. "This will take some time. Tamra, I suggest that Budra and I stay in Corsica, when Xento brings the spacecraft back to Versailles."

'I agree," said Tamra. "Thern, Pixel, and I will wait in the cottage until Xento returns with the spacecraft. We have to think of a way to get Sylvie's father back from Paris."

When the three Larthans left for Corsica Tamra explained to Thern why Sylvie's father had not returned from Paris. "If you and Adam do find Sylvie's father you will have to encourage him to return home. She will need someone to care for her when, I hope, I have cured the brain damage."

"Adam should be a great help," said Pixel. "He is still struggling with French but his tutor can help to locate Rene. If you can find Rene then Adam could rent horses, Paris is only twenty miles from Versailles."

"But Rene should not be told about Sylvie until she is returned to the cottage." Tamra cautioned.

"I understand," said Thern. "When I have found Rene I will return here to consult with Pixel."

"We will wait until you return with Sylvie." Pixel assured Tamra. "We should also be concerned about the loan to Count Avide. Tomorrow I am going to ask David to find out more about the Count. It would be helpful, Tamra, if you could give us a tour of the palace tonight. With David's help tomorrow I might find out where Count Avide lives."

Thern had more questions about Sylvie's father before Tamra took them for a tour of the palace. They had more discussions at the cottage about Count Avide and how they might repay the loan. Pixel suggested, jokingly, that he might fly to New Orleans for more pirate's treasure. Tamra reminded him that, sadly, the treasure was gone.

When Xento returned with the spacecraft he found it quite easy to load the bed to the undercarriage. His robotic tools worked smoothly. But tying Sylvie to the bed with rope was almost impossible for the tiny Larthans! Looping the rope around Sylvie was easy enough but trying to knot the two strands of rope was problematic. Four Larthans working together were not strong enough to make a knot that would hold. Xento ultimately solved the problem by using the tractor's robotic arm to hold the ends of the rope together while the Larthans tightened the knot.

Tamra insisted on flying in the bed with Sylvie. "I just want to be there in case of an emergency. I can radio you, Xento, if I think the spacecraft is going too fast."

"I understand, Tamra," said Xento. "I had planned to fly quite slowly and at a low altitude so that it would not be too cold for Sylvie. Your radio feedback will help me maintain the right speed."

To avoid the high mountains in the south of France Xento flew the spacecraft down the Rhone river valley to the Mediterranean Sea, then followed the coast to Nice before heading south to their home base on Corsica. The trip took over four hours, and Tamra slept most of the way. Once she had established the right speed with Xento there was nothing for her to do. She snuggled close to Sylvie's face so that she could hear her breathing and was soon fast asleep. It had been a busy day.

As soon as they landed Tamra assumed her role of emergency doctor. She set up the intravenous feeding system and showed Budra and Greida how to replenish the flow with the barrels of nutrient that they had prepared. Xento helped her to take the hundreds of x-ray images she needed to determine the nature of Sylvie's injury. Once she had a computer image of the damaged area she released tiny pellets into the blood vessels leading to the brain. On her monitor she could direct the pellets, somewhat like a modern computer game, to the problem area in

Sylvie's brain. The pellets would fire, on her command, energy rays that would dissolve the blockage. She worked through the night and before sunrise she was confident that she had eliminated the blockage.

"It will take some time for Sylvie to recover," she told her admiring compatriots. "I have already seen a response from Sylvie. She moved her finger when I tickled her hand."

"Congratulations, Tamra!' said Pixel. 'We are all proud of you. Should I tell David that Sylvie will be returning home tonight? I am leaving now to meet him at the cottage."

"Absolutely. I want to get her back to the cottage before she regains consciousness. We should plan to be there as soon as it gets dark. I hope that David can spend the night with her. And perhaps we can get her father to return home soon. Sylvie will need their support when she regains consciousness."

Flying at top speed Pixel arrived at the cottage in less than an hour. David was in the cottage when Pixel flew in through an open window. "I have good news, David. Sylvie is recovering. Tamra will be bringing Sylvie home tonight. She would like you to spend the night with Sylvie. Can you stay tonight?"

David was relieved to see Pixel. He had spent a sleepless night worrying about Sylvie and the tiny creatures who seemed so confident that they could help her. He had questions of his own. "That is good news, Pixel. I can stay tonight. But I am very confused. We have time now, could you tell me where you and Tamra come from?"

Before Pixel could respond there was a loud threatening knock at the cottage door.

David was very alarmed. "What should we do?'

"I'll hide!" said Pixel.

At that moment two nobles burst into the room. Pixel flew quickly to the wooden beam that supported the cottage roof. He could see that one of the men was very angry with David. The man was shouting harsh words at David. Pixel had never studied French so he could not understand what the noble was saying. David was quietly defiant in his answers. Suddenly the noble pulled his sword from its scabbard and pointed it at David. Pixel was about to make a diversionary lunge at the noble when he saw David backing away from the sword and out the cottage door. The noble followed, sword in hand, and pointed David towards the palace. Disconsolately David trudged through the woods to Versailles. Pixel watched the two men search the cottage before riding away on their horses.

David was seething with anger when Pixel caught up with him.

"Who was that? I thought he was going to kill you!"

"Count Avide! A monster! He was looking for Sylvie. He had the Sherriff with him. He wanted to deliver a notice saying that she and her father would be evicted because the loan was not repaid. I told him that I had not seen Sylvie for two days."

"But why did he threaten to kill you?"

"He knows that I'm English, and that my father was hired by the king. He said that the king was stupid for hiring an English gardener. He said I was lying about Sylvie, he had seen her himself yesterday; he was in the fox hunt. I'm not sure why he was so angry. When he drew his sword the Sheriff told him not to be foolish. I think he just wanted to frighten me."

"David, be calm. Tell me more about your father. Why did the King hire him?"

"My dad worked as a gardener for the King of England at his palace in Kew. He was very creative; he became very skilled at pruning and shaping plants so that they looked like animals. Somehow the King of France learned about this and decided he would like animal shaped plants in the Versailles gardens. My dad was asked if he would go to Versailles, as sort of a peace gesture to France. He was offered a very good salary, our own apartment in the palace, and our meals in the king's kitchen. My father thought it would be a good opportunity for me to learn French."

"So your father meets with the King of France?"

"No, the King doesn't meet with commoners. I think he met the King just once, when we came here four years ago."

"What do you know about Count Avide? Have you seen him before?"

"I don't know him. But I have a friend in the palace who may be able to tell me about Count Avide."

"That's a good idea, David. Try to find out where the count lives. I assume that he has an apartment somewhere in the palace. I would like to explore his apartment."

David was getting very distressed. "I'm not sure how I can help Sylvie now. Should I take a chance and come to see Sylvie tonight?"

"I think you should. If you can find out where the Count lives my friends and I can watch out for him while you visit with Sylvie. We will find some way to stop him."

"I'll do everything I can. Where should we meet?"

"I thought we could meet in your apartment. But you will have to help me find the way. When we get to the palace grounds I will sit on your shoulder while you walk towards the building where your apartment is located. Try to avoid other people, but don't worry too much, I can fly away very quickly. When you get to your building point out your apartment, and if there is a window open I will fly in and meet you inside."

"Pixel, I hope one day you will tell me more about your people. Right now I just want to tell you that I think you are a very clever little man!"

"Thank you, David. And I think you are a very brave young man."

The King's servants lived in a large two storied building near the palace gate. David's apartment was on the second floor; small, but comfortably furnished.

"This will be our base," said Pixel when he met with David. "While you are trying to find out about Count Avide I will be exploring the apartments in the royal compound. I will fly back here frequently to see you."

Pixel was very concerned about Count Avide. He felt it was unlikely that the Count would come to the cottage at night time. But if the Count came during the day Pixel had no idea how they could protect Sylvie. Pixel knew enough about humans to realize that the Count would not show mercy for a peasant, even someone as defenceless as Sylvie.

The huge conference room, adjoining the King's bedroom, was filled with nobles, all foppishly dressed, with elaborate wigs and elegant tights. Pixel flew from one glittering chandelier to another, looking for Count Avide. When the long meeting ended, and there was no sign of Count Avide, Pixel followed the King to his private workshop. It was said of the king that he loved the French people dearly but was not a strong leader; he could not control the selfish French nobles. He preferred to spend time in his workshop. When Pixel saw how happy the king was with his favourite hobby, making locks, he understood why the king was so anxious to leave the bedlam in his bedroom.

Pixel was returning to David's apartment when he received a radio signal from Thern indicating that he was returning to Versailles. He flew quickly to the cottage to meet Thern.

"Sylvie's grandfather is dead!" exclaimed Thern, as he flew into the cottage.

Pixel was shocked. "Are you sure?'

"Quite sure, Pixel. Adam and I found the bake shop this morning. The front door was closed and there was a sign in the window which read: 'Shop closed because of death in the family.' The small living room in the back of the shop was crowded with well wishers. I did not feel comfortable in the room. I looked quickly in an adjoining room and saw the body of Sylvie's grandfather lying in an open casket. I didn't want to stay. I radioed you and talked to Adam. He wants to know if there is anything that he can do to help. It is very sad!"

"Very sad! And very complicated! We will have to tell David. Fly with me, Thern, I want you to meet David. Tell him what you saw."

David was quite happy to meet another one of Tamra's friends. He had news of his own, but he listened quietly while Thern talked about the death of Sylvie's grandfather.

"I am not surprised," said David. "Sylvie told me that her grandfather is quite old. He is much older than his wife."

David handed Pixel a map of the palace grounds. "My friend, Henri, made this map for me. I think it is easy to follow. He also introduced me to his grandfather who is a retired valet. His name is Gilbert and he has worked all of his life in the palace. Gilbert knows all about the intrigues of the King's nobles. He told me that the nobles speak quite openly about private matters while they are attended to by their servants. He was anxious to tell me shocking stories that he had heard during the previous king's reign. I had to interrupt him several times before I could get him to focus on Count Avide. Gilbert never worked for the Count but knows about him. The Count has a very minor role at the palace. He buys land for the King from farmers who own land within or adjacent to the King's hunting ground. The King would like to buy all the farms within his hunting forest. Gilbert is quite sure that the Count is deceiving the King."

"How does Gilbert know this?" asked Pixel.

"Gilbert has a friend, another valet, who overheard the Count discussing the scheme with the sheriff. It's very complicated, mortgages, illegal bills of sale signed by the sheriff, false invoices. Gilbert is a very intelligent man and he carefully explained the details of the fraud. But I really did not understand it until he gave me a simple example. Are you interested Pixel?"

"Yes, I am. I have an idea and knowing more about the Count would help me. Just give us the example."

"I will give it a try," said David. "Let's assume that a farmer is willing to sell his farm to the King for one thousand French francs. Since the King does not have time to deal with such details he has given Count Avide the right to negotiate with all such farmers. And the King will pay the Count a fee of say ten percent on all such purchases. So if the Count buys a property for one thousand francs he will earn a fee from the King of one hundred francs, ten percent of the price of the property. The King would pay a total of one thousand, one hundred francs for the property;

one thousand francs would be paid to the farmer and one hundred francs would be paid to the Count. Does this make sense, Pixel?"

"I understand. But I can see that Thern is mystified. Thern I will explain all this to you later. David please tell us more."

David continued, "Assume that the Count had loaned this farmer five hundred francs and the farmer was unable to repay the loan. What the Count should do is offer to buy the property for the King so that he can pay himself the five hundred francs owed to him and give five hundred francs to the farmer. Instead what the Count tries to do is force the farmer to abandon the farm for not paying the loan. He uses the sheriff to threaten the farmers. If the farmer abandons the property the Count sells the property to the King but keeps all the money for himself. In essence he is defrauding the farmer of five hundred francs."

"I understand perfectly." said Pixel. "You are right, David, the Count is deceiving the King. Why don't the servants report this to the King?"

"They are afraid of losing their jobs. A servant at the palace is much better off than most French commoners. Besides who could they report it to? Who could they trust? The Count is not the only corrupt noble at the palace. From what Gilbert told me there are many nobles who are defrauding the King."

Pixel was quite thoughtful for several minutes. "David, I have an idea. But it might put you in danger. I want you to think carefully about my proposal. I believe it's the only way we can stop the Count from evicting Sylvie and her father from their farm."

"I will risk my life to save Sylvie!"

"Let's talk about the plan, David. If we are careful, there may be no danger. My idea is that you write a letter to the King telling him about Sylvie's accident and the fact that she and her father are going to be evicted by the Count. You would not sign your name to the letter. Thern and I will deliver the letter to the King. We will take it to the King's bedroom late tonight and put it in a place where he is sure to see it when he wakes up. I understand that the King really wants to help the French people. He may not be interested in complicated economic proposals but he loves the French people. If that is true he just might send someone to help Sylvie and stop the Count. What do you think, David?"

"It's a great idea, Pixel. But what would we do if the King simply gives the letter to one of his ministers, a minister who is a friend of the Count's?"

"That's the key question David, and that is the danger. If the King does not help Sylvie my friends and I might have to move her again. If your life is in danger we will protect you. We can take you back to England if necessary. Or we could take you and Sylvie to another country. Your life would change dramatically. Are you prepared to take the risk?"

"I'm ready Pixel. What's the next step?"

"You should start drafting the letter to the King. Show us where the Count's apartment is on your map. Thern and I will visit the Count. We will return here in an hour or so to finalize our plan."

On Corsica Tamra was anxious to get Sylvie back to the cottage. She was worried that Sylvie might open her eyes during the flight. She imagined Sylvie's terror if she awoke to find herself flying, and unable to move. Tamra decided to cover Sylvie's eyes with a mask for the return flight. She cut a strip of cloth from Sylvie's blanket and, with the help of the others, draped it over Sylvie's eyes and tucked the ends under Sylvie's ears. Budra and Greida insisted on flying back on the bed with Tamra and Sylvie. "To help keep the mask down," they said. But it was really for the thrill of the ride! Tamra radioed Pixel just before they landed at the cottage, she wanted David there so that he could start talking to Sylvie. She wanted to be sure that Sylvie would recover.

The Larthans were joyous when they saw David kneel by Sylvie's bedside and with his first word—Sylvie—they saw a quiet smile on her face!

They hugged and congratulated Tamra, and danced with glee on the kitchen table.

Pixel, always the serious one, thought that this was an historic moment for Larthans on Earth—they had saved the life of a human. But he also realized that tomorrow would be a critical day. It was time to tell Tamra and the other Larthans about Count Avide, and the plan to seek the King's help.

When Pixel had outlined the plan Xento asked, "What do we do, Pixel, if the King does not help Sylvie?"

"David, Thern and I discussed that possibility," Pixel replied. "We have ideas, but no real plan. It depends on Count Avide and what action he takes. If he learns that the King received a note about Sylvie the Count may very well try to do harm to David. Thern will be watching the Count all day tomorrow. If the Count rides towards the cottage Thern will fly here and warn David. We think that David should stay at the cottage tonight. He has left a note with his father telling him that he has to help a friend and will be away for several days. David has a married sister who lives in the south of England. If David is in danger we could fly him there."

"So we should keep the spacecraft nearby?" asked Xento.

"Yes, Xento, until we know the Count's plans."

Tamra asked, "And what about Sylvie? Who will care for her?"

"We need advice from you, Tamra," said Pixel. "We have suggested to David that we could fly both he and Sylvie to England. Is she healthy enough to make another flight?"

"I would much prefer that she stay in the cottage," said Tamra. "You can see how well she is responding to David's voice. Pixel, would Count Avide really hurt a defenceless girl?"

"I don't know, Tamra. That's why we will have to wait and see. We may also be able to encourage her father to come home. We would only move Sylvie if we had no other options."

"Right now David's presence is vital to Sylvie's recovery. If he has to fly to England then I would want Sylvie to fly with him."

"I understand, Tamra," said Pixel. "We will do everything we can to keep Sylvie and David together, in the cottage."

The discussion continued for a while before Pixel said, "Thern and I need a few hours sleep. We have an important meeting with the King of France tonight."

It was after midnight when Pixel and Thern flew to David's apartment to pick up the King's note. It was hidden beneath David's bed. The message was on a single piece of paper, rolled tightly, and tied with a piece of string. The ends of the string were long enough for Pixel and Thern to grasp easily as they flew with the note to the King's bedroom. They rested the note on the edge of the window before exploring the bedroom. There were no servants in the room, but one of the King's guardsmen was on duty outside the bedroom. The King's bed was an enormous four poster, with richly embroidered curtains on three sides. Pixel flew over the bedstead to ensure that the King was asleep before they flew in with the note. They had brought an extra length of string to attach to the roof of the bed's canopy so that the string hung down to the middle of the King's bed, with the note attached. It would be the first thing that the King would see when he awoke.

They also had a video machine which Pixel used to project a single image of Sylvie's face, directly above the sleeping king. Her eyes were closed in a smile of contentment.

Thern landed on the bed, close to the Kings' ear. He whispered to the King, in French, "If the good king loves his people he should save this French girl." He repeated the same phrase, louder each time, until the King was awakened.

What the King thought he saw, when he opened his eyes in the darkened bedroom, was the floating face of an angel! Pixel stopped projecting Sylvie's image as soon as he was sure that the King had seen it. The King was quite startled by the dream; he lit a bedside candle to regain his confidence. And then he saw the note. He was very agitated by what he read, and it was difficult for him to fall asleep. When he did fall asleep Pixel and Thern repeated their video/ voice-over dream until the King was wakened again. This time he was too upset to go back to sleep.

The King's two top advisors were quite surprised at how aggressive he was when they met with him for the normal breakfast meeting. Usually he would listen quietly to their proposals and invariably agreed with their recommendations. Today he just wanted to take them for a ride in the woods. He cancelled the morning meeting with the nobles.

The King loved hunting and horse riding in his forest, perhaps more than lock making. He knew exactly where to find the cottage described in the mysterious letter. He dismounted quickly when he arrived at the cottage and stopped at the door to read a notice that had been posted there by the sheriff. He pulled the notice from the door and handed it to his prime minister.

"Read that aloud!" said the King.

His adviser was quite shocked by the King's behaviour, but did as he was told. 'This is a notice to the residents of this building that they must vacate this property within ten days. They will be evicted as squatters if they do not leave by that date. Signed, Sheriff of Versailles.'

"Do you know of this?" asked the King.

"No, your majesty," his aide replied. "This is the responsibility of Count Avide."

David now opened the cottage door and bowed respectfully to the King. "May I be of assistance, your majesty?"

"Do you own this property, young man?"

"No, your majesty. I am caring for the owner's daughter. She was injured in an accident. Would you like to see her your majesty?"

When the King walked in and saw Sylvie in the bed he knew instantly that this was the angel in his dreams. How could this be? A sign from the heavens? What did it mean? He turned to David. "What do you know about this girl?"

"Her name is Sylvie. I just met her a few weeks ago. Her father is in Paris, he is trying to raise money to pay a debt that he owes to Count Avide."

"Count Avide!" The King was suddenly very angry. Everything that he read in the mysterious note was true. The Count was a scoundrel! He turned to his two ministers. "Order Count Avide to quit the palace immediately! Tell him that I no longer trust him. Tell him that I have forgiven the debt owed by this farmer. And I want you to arrest the sheriff. If he has been defrauding me then he should be imprisoned."

"I will follow your instructions, your majesty." said the prime minister.

"And I want the father of this girl brought from Paris immediately. I expect to see him here when I visit his daughter tomorrow. Send soldiers to search Paris if necessary!"

"Excuse me your majesty," said David. "I have a letter with the address of Sylvie's father."

The King took the letter from David, "Do I know you, young man? I think I have seen you before."

"My name is David, your majesty. I am the son of your English gardener."

"Yes, now I remember," said the King. "Your French is very good, David. Will you be staying with Sylvie until her father returns?"

"Yes, I will, your majesty."

"I will return tomorrow. You are a fine young man," said the King, as he rode off with his ministers.

When David told the Larthans what the King said they all started dancing gleefully on the kitchen table. Shouting, laughing and congratulating each other.

Tamra hugged Pixel so fiercely, and so meaningfully, that he knew that this was not just an historic moment for the Larthans. It was a new beginning for Tamra and him.

EPILOGUE

The King's men brought Sylvie's father and grandmother home to the cottage in grand style; in one of the King's coaches. They were still mourning the death of Sylvie's grandfather and had not yet reopened the bake shop. David told them all about Sylvie's accident, except for the role of the Larthans. He told them that he had asked one of the King's chamber maids to hide the note in the King's bed. Rene was very impressed with the courage of David and it was quite obvious to him that the young Englishman cared deeply for Sylvie.

In the first few days Rene and Sylvie's grandmother slept at the cottage and every evening David was able to return to his apartment at the palace. Tamra would look in secretly on Sylvie during the night and would have a meeting each morning with David to give him medical advice.

Sylvie opened her eyes on the third day. She was able to reply to questions by blinking her eyes but she had not yet recovered the ability to speak. Tamra told David that it would take time and therapy for Sylvie to fully recover. Rene and Sylvie's grandmother were anxious to return to Paris to get the bake shop started again, it was their only source of income. The King had promised to buy the cottage and farm but Rene decided to defer selling the farm until Sylvie was well enough to be moved to Paris. David volunteered to look after Sylvie until she was fully recovered and so Rene and Sylvie's grandmother were able to return to the bake shop. Tamra was delighted with this arrangement. It gave her daily access to Sylvie.

The Larthans agreed that Sylvie should be told about their role in saving her life. David told her the story slowly, over a period of several days, before he finally introduced Tamra. Sylvie's delight at meeting the tiny creature who had saved her life seemed to spur her recovery. She was soon talking excitedly, but with a slight slur. Tamra and David developed a routine that hastened Sylvie's recovery. First, in English, Tamra would say something about life on Larth. David would translate what Tamra said into French, and Sylvie would repeat what David said. It made Sylvie's therapy fun, taught her and David about life on Larth, and helped Tamra to learn French. Sylvie was fully recovered by the end of that summer and she joined her father and grandmother at the bake shop in Paris. The King had been very generous in the price he paid for the farm so Rene had enough money to build Sylvie her own bedroom on the second floor of the bake shop, and to expand his bakery.

David also moved to Paris; he stayed at Adam's apartment and became his French tutor. They became great friends. Pixel's weekly meetings with Adam now included Tamra and David. The discussions focused on the economic crisis in France. David became very concerned about the poverty he saw in the streets of Paris. He had seen many beggars in London but they were fewer in number, and docile compared to the angry menacing paupers in Paris. David soon realized that he had a passion for politics. He wanted to learn how governments could be improved to eliminate poverty. He eventually found a job translating French newspaper articles into English for publication in London newspapers, and he helped Adam prepare his reports for Mary's newspaper in Boston. Tamra would often fly with Pixel to Boston. Mary and Sally adored her, and Bill teased her incessantly.

Tamra visited Sylvie several times a week at the bakery. She was delighted when Sylvie expressed an interest in becoming a doctor. Tamra used video images of Sylvie's brain and other primary organs to explain the functions of the body. Sylvie worked as a nurse at a Paris hospital and obtained all the current medical books. Tamra reviewed these books with Sylvie and was able to confirm for Sylvie the medical procedures that were valid and those that were false. Sylvie was apprenticed to a doctor when she was nineteen; he soon realized that she was more knowledgeable than most of the doctors in Paris.

David and Sylvie were married in 1789, in a simple service at the Paris Town Hall. Adam and the Larthans attended a private wedding party in David's apartment. It was a truly joyous affair.

France was in turmoil in 1789. The King and his advisers had tried to get the rich nobles to pay more taxes to prevent the country from becoming bankrupt. But they had selfishly refused to help. Ordinary citizens, angry and disillusioned with the King and his nobles, decided to set up their own government, a government without a King, a government like the United States of America. It was ironical that the King of France, who had helped the American Colonies in their revolt against the King Of England, should now suffer the same fate from his own people.

David, who would be forever thankful to the King of France for saving Sylvie's life, understood that the French people were justified in their revolution against the monarchy. But he could not understand why the revolutionary government authorized the execution of the King. As a news reporter he had to watch as the King was taken to a scaffold and beheaded by a guillotine. That night, with Sylvie by his side, David cried uncontrollably. Sylvie could not console him. He remembered the King as a decent human being, an ordinary man who loved the French people.

Budra and Greida had a very difficult time trying to convince Pixel that he should ask Tamra to be his wife. They started their campaign of persuasion when Tamra had told them, as is the custom on Larth, that she would like to be courted by Pixel. It was a Larthan custom, based on the inherent trait of Larthans not to offend, that women should tell their friends when they wished to be courted by a man. By custom her friends tell the chosen young man that his overtures would not be refused. This avoided the embarrassment a young man would feel to be rejected by a woman. Pixel retorted that Tamra really had no choice; he was after all the only available Larthan male on Earth. Furthermore he was sure she must be offended by Mission Control who had in reality chosen her to be his mate. He did not want to be part of a scheme that was making her do something against her wishes. Budra reminded Pixel that Tamra had spent three years travelling in a spacecraft knowing that Pixel was the only Larthan male on Earth. "Why would she travel all that distance if she didn't like you in some way?" she asked.

"For the adventure." Pixel replied. "That's exactly why I came here."

In truth Pixel was very shy in such matters. Tamra understood this more clearly than did Budra and Greida. She was not at all concerned, as they were, at Pixel's reluctance to speak of romance. And so, on a memorably beautiful spring day in Paris, when Pixel finally had the courage to tell Tamra how much he cared for her, she guided him gently through what he considered to be very dangerous waters.

Tamra and Pixel decided that the wedding should take place in Boston. Since it would be the first Larthan marriage on Earth they thought it should be carefully planned. Budra and Greida, with help from Mary and Sally, designed the wedding service; it was a combination of the traditions of both planets.

The attic of the sea captain's house was filled with flowers for the wedding. The Larthan planes were parked on the deck overlooking Boston harbour. The service was held on a desk that was normally covered with charts. Bill was Pixel's best man, Sally was the flower girl, and Budra was the bridesmaid. The taking of vows was administered by Thern. The vow

was similar to the one that Mary and Bill made at their wedding, with one

small change. The Larthans thought the phrase in the vow, 'love, honour

and obey' should be changed to 'love, honour and be happy.'

A video of the wedding was sent to Mission Control; it absolutely

thrilled the proud parents of the bride and groom.

2050

◄━━ ⊰◆⊱ ━━►

By the beginning of the twenty-first century there was over one hundred thousand Larthans living on Earth. They lived in mountain top communities, far from humans. They had not been in contact with humans for over one hundred years. When humans invented the telephone and created crude flying machines Larthans decided it would be impossible to keep their existence on Earth a secret if they continued to make contact with individual humans. By this time Larthans had learned all of the world's major languages. There was always a small group of Larthans who thought that they could help humans by teaching them how to use solar power efficiently. But the majority of Larthans thought that humans should be allowed to develop technology at their own pace. They were concerned about the warring nature of humans. The tribal instincts of humans seemed to make war inevitable. Larthans were concerned that they could somehow become involved in a human war and be themselves annihilated. The Larthan consensus was that they should to wait for humans to mature as nations and learn to live in peace. Larthans could then be assured that their technological help would be used for all mankind.

Larthans discussed these issues in an annual convention that they held on a remote island in the Pacific Ocean. Global warming now became the primary issue at these conventions.

Larthans were at first encouraged when governments accepted the warnings of their scientists that global warming was a dire threat to the planet. They hoped that the worldwide expansion of the internet would encourage humans to work together to avoid the impending crisis. When governments failed to deal with the threat Larthans were dismayed.

In 2050 the Statue of Liberty was still standing proudly in New York harbour, even though Liberty Island itself was ten feet under water. Global warming had caused the polar ice caps to melt much sooner than scientists had predicted and rising sea levels had inundated all of the world's coastal cities. The skyscrapers on Manhattan Island were empty. The roads and the subway system were undersea; New Yorkers had fled to higher ground.

Some coastal cities in rich countries had developed plans to evacuate their citizens when sea levels rose. But in poorer coastal cities there were no evacuation plans and the millions who fled the rising waters became homeless refugees.

Global warming resulted in worldwide water shortages, and oil became so expensive that it had to be rationed. Countries fought futile wars with nuclear weapons to control the dwindling supply of oil and water. People lost faith in their governments. When national governments collapsed, so did businesses of all kinds. Money became useless. Millions died as people fought each other for the food that remained in supermarkets, farmer's barns, and warehouses.

In North America and other developed countries many people had anticipated the collapse of governments. They used the internet to set up alternative forms of local governments to prepare themselves for a future without oil, electricity or tap water. In the suburbs lawns were converted into vegetable gardens. Swimming pools, rain filled from the roofs of houses, became community reservoirs. Solar panels were installed on all houses to provide heat in the winter. Garages were converted into greenhouses so that food could be grown all year round. People raised chickens in their yards, vegetables were planted in public parks, and abandoned industrial farms were converted into community gardens. Local communities bartered food with each other, bicycles being the prime means of transport. These communities survived, barely, when electricity was no longer available and the internet died.

It was a an unimaginable catastrophe for city dwellers in poor countries. Millions fled to the countryside to seek food from poor farmers whose crops had been decimated by droughts. There were very few survivors as people fought with each other for food and water.

When societies ceased to function Larthans decided that it was time to help. They would share their solar power expertise with humans. They hoped that the humans who survived the global warming catastrophe would be motivated to rebuild their communities with a new philosophy. They hoped that humans would use Larthan technology to make everyone happy, not to make weapons of war and some people rich. They hoped that sharing, not greed, would become the prime motivator for humans. They hoped that humans were ready to live rich lives with a profound respect for the natural world. Their hopes became a struggle.

CPSIA information can be obtained at www.ICGtesting.com
Printed in the USA
LVOW122053220313

325654LV00002B/43/P